Sheila Kohler is the author of the novels *Cracks*, *Crossways*, and *The Children of Pithiviers*, among others, and she has contributed articles to a wide variety of magazines and literary journals. Born in South Africa, she currently lives in New York City and teaches at Princeton. This is her seventh novel. —

Becoming Jane Eyre

Sheila Kohler

corsair

Constable & Robinson Ltd
3 The Lanchesters
162 Fulham Palace Road
London W6 9ER
www.constablerobinson.com

First published by Penguin Group, 2009

This edition published by Corsair,
an imprint of Constable & Robinson Ltd, 2011

A copy of the British Library Cataloguing in
Publication data is available from the British Library

ISBN 978-1-84901-086-3

Printed and bound in the UK

1 3 5 7 9 10 8 6 4 2

To the love of my life, my husband Bill

VOLUME ONE

✿ ✿

Manchester
1846

CHAPTER ONE

Father and Daughter

*H*e wakes to the scratching of a pencil against a page: a noise out of the darkness. He lies quite still on his back, reaching out for sound. His ears have become wings, straining, stretching, carrying him away. The world comes to him only through sound, and there is precious little of that.

Even the sounds of quiet Boundary Street on the outskirts of this large industrial town are strange to him. Apart from the scratching, he can hear little except an occasional cry, the rumble of carriage wheels below, the call of a city bird. He hungers for the wild sounds of his hill-village home: the low keening of the wind over moors, the bark of a dog, the cries of crows, the tolling of his church bell.

He misses the sights of his world: the sweep of a lonely hill; the joy of an eagle, plummeting wildly through the blue air in search of food for his young. Now he is a bird with wounded wing. Is he cast forever *into bottomless perdition*? Is he to dwell in *Adamantine Chains and penal Fire?* He learned to recite Milton to himself as a child, and the words come easily to him now. In the darkness he feels the heat of the poem.

He imagines opening the front door of his parsonage, the light streaming in from the window over the stairs and the mad scrabble of paws coming to greet him across the stone floor. In his mind he holds Keeper or little spoiled Flossy, the black-and-white King Charles spaniel, in his arms. He can smell their wild smells of grass and wind, from the moors. He even misses the canary, singing in its cage, and Emily's geese. He has walked for hours with the dogs. Striding fast across the hills, through the dark heath, in all sorts of weather has warmed his blood and his heart and become a wellspring of his verse. His children are fond of all kinds of animals, and so is he, but of course the dogs have not followed him here.

Not even the sound of church bells, chiming the hours, comes to him in this part of town. He imagines the chimes, which have regulated his days and nights for so long, calling him to his God, who has not forsaken him, surely. He will find his way to the light of Heaven again, surely.

Is it early morning? How long has he been lying here? This immobility, this helplessness, this perpetual darkness, are too hard to bear. *God help me!*

All his life he has marched onward, striding upward, acquiring knowledge, position, and distinction, going on with hope and firmness of purpose and conviction in the Army of the Lord, carrying the Word of the Lord like a banner before him to sinners and sufferers, with the belief in his heart that he brings salvation. He remembers how he joined the Home

Guard at Cambridge as a young man to protect England from the unruly French – a warrior priest.

But now they have nailed his sixty-nine-year-old bones to his couch. They have pierced his eyes with a crown of thorns. He has become a blind mouth. How much longer will he have to lie here helplessly in the silence of the late-summer darkness, with nothing but the sound of a scratching pencil in his ears? Will his mind survive its creeping dimness? There is only a thin sheet over his body, but his bones feel heavy. Despite the hot, dry air he is cold, cold.

He recites the familiar words from the 23rd Psalm: *Yea, though I walk through the valley of the shadow of death, yet shall I fear no evil. Thy rod and thy staff they comfort me. The Lord is my shepherd, I shall not want.* He repeats the words as he did when he lay awake and conscious under the knife.

They propped his eye open with some steel instrument as the cruel work was done. Two of them held on to him, should he struggle, but he did not, lying still as death, in his God's hands, excruciatingly conscious of the knife's work in that delicate place, of every sound in the room, and of the presence sitting quietly in a corner, a comfort to him: Charlotte.

High on the flat, white bed, her father lies. She sits by his side on a low ottoman near the marble chimneypiece, writing in the silence and the half dark of the early morning. They have found convenient lodgings. Her father's room opens into hers, and there is a small sitting room to which she can retreat. The nurse, a redheaded woman in her late twenties or early thirties who is lodged upstairs in one of the third-floor rooms, is competent, if annoyingly officious. Charlotte hears her clomping down the stairs. The doctor has been helpful in this, as he has in all things. Though not large, their rooms are comfortable. She props her writing desk on her knees and places a small candle at her side to light her page.

Against the wall a monstrous wardrobe looms ominously. To her right the curtained windows give onto the street, and between them a dim mirror stands. The doctor has ordered privation of light and perfect silence. The strangeness of these lodgings, the dryness of the dusty air, the hot darkness, and the suffering presence beside her make her shiver.

Next door she hears the nurse moving about with purpose, dropping things on the floor. Living in such proximity, she has taken a dislike to the large, hard-faced woman who enters the room in her navy uniform, her round, white cap with its ribbons flowing down her back, her black stockings brushing together with a sigh.

Charlotte nods her head in response to her greeting. The nurse's presence is an intrusion she attempts to ignore. She prefers to listen to her father's breathing, to be alone with him. A distant, God-fearing man preoccupied with his Christian duty, his concern for his large, poor parish, his grief, and his only boy, she has never been alone with him like this.

The nurse asks how she is feeling this morning. She replies that her tooth aches, that sleep seems to have abandoned her. The nurse suggests a walk, in a voice that sounds loud and shrill. Charlotte shakes her head. She has little desire to walk in these charmless, suffocating streets.

How much walking she has done in her life! She has scampered as a child on the moors for the joy of it, the freedom, the escape from the cramped house, the adults' oppressive presence. She has walked for necessity, for exercise, for pleasure, and for the beauty of the natural world around her. She has walked to tire herself out. Here, she prefers the time alone with her father in the early morning, before the nurse comes bustling into the room, moments of escape into the world of imagination. Here, she is able to let her mind go where it will, even while her eye is fixed on him.

She lifts her gaze from the page, where she has written words and crossed them out. She surveys the scene. Things seem very still to her and, oddly, in the darkened room she now seems to see more clearly. It is being alone with her father, being his eyes and his hands and even his voice, his link with life, that brings this clarity.

She finds herself drifting into a moment of reflection. It is difficult to fix the boundaries between imagination and memory. She absorbs what comes to her, drawing images into this dim, silent space. All the small objects in the room – the bulb-shaped water bottle, the green counterpane, the plant on the windowsill – seem to mean something. She is in a moment of transition. She looks for signs of what she will become.

She was glad to come here on her own with her father, yet reluctant to leave her brother and her two sisters at home. What will happen there? Will her sisters find the time, the courage, to work on their new books? All through the summer, before she came to Manchester, they took their desks out into the garden, to work in the shade of the cherry tree. What mischief will her brother be making? She sees him, sitting in his study, his head in his hands, an empty bottle before him, raving about a woman called Misery who follows him everywhere, a woman he calls his wife.

Shudders run through her father's body, as they did through hers as a child when he would shoot his pistol at dawn, as though a shock has run through him.

'What?' she asks. 'What is it?' She reaches a hand to still his beating heart. She has never been able to stare at him like this, touch him freely in the muted light. He reaches out for her. What does he know of her, or she of him, after all these years? What secrets would he tell her if he could speak? Would she want to hear them? What would he say about his marriage, his parents, his God? Had he chosen her mother for love or for her superior position in society, the fifty pounds a year? Or was it her religion? Did he want her help with his work in the church? Did he think she could advance his career? Was his religion simply a means of advancing socially?

But he only asks for water, as he does repeatedly. He has always been a thirsty man. Though he is president of the local Temperance Society, she is not sure he has not used alcohol for more than medicinal purposes.

She pours the water, resumes her seat, and takes up her pencil and her square notebook again, as though tied to her post beside him.

-ℰ-

On her return home from Brussels after New Year's Day, burdened with her own sadness, she was appalled to find her father so helpless. Blind, like his beloved Milton, he could not venture outside in the snow because the glare hurt his eyes. Full of pity and terror, as well as impatience at his helplessness, she was obliged to lead him through the narrow streets to visit his parishioners and to read and write and see for him, describing the landscape she knows so well, the fields, the sky, and snow. In his thankfulness he showed her more consideration than he had ever done, accepted her help and love, yielded to her attendance on him.

Each evening when they sat together, she brought up the good chance of having his eyesight improved by the operation. All through the winter and spring she worked on him. He procrastinated, finding excuses. Finally she persuaded him to go through with it. Was this wise? Was she being selfish or merely dutiful? Was her motivation one of revenge?

She relives the scene: two men in white at his side, like the flaming angels she had seen as a child, standing at the head of her youngest sister's cradle, but here prepared to wrestle with her father, their hands on his shoulders, pinning him down. The glint of the scalpel. She holds her breath, unable to avert her terrified yet fascinated gaze as the surgeon cuts through the cornea. She watches her father's face contort with agony and hears the cry escape his lips. Afterward, she needs the arm of one of the assistants to take her from the room.

Now her mouth is dry, her lips chapped, her bowels blocked. She puts her hand to her cheek, feeling her flaking skin. What will the future bring for them all? Will this let in the light? What would they all do without him, he who provides the rent-free house, the yearly stipend?

It is this which clothes, feeds, and shelters them. They are entirely dependent on him. Without him they would all be separated again, scattered to earn their bread in the professions they all hate and have failed at abysmally: teaching, tutoring, and, in the brother's case, clerking on the railways. Their livelihood, the roof over their heads, their beloved parsonage, all will be taken from them at his demise, perpetual curacy holding only so long as the curate lives.

Will she be the one to save them all from penury with a new book, when her first one, her *Professor*, has just been rejected? She cannot believe it was without merit. Her soul is marked on every page. She is each one of her characters: the two brothers who are estranged, as were so often the ones in her own brother's tales. She can still hear their voices, see their faces, feel their forms. She hears the wicked brother's wife, Mrs Edward Crimsworth, say with her lively lisp, 'You are late.' She hears the swish of Edward's whip. The child, Victor Crimsworth, has her brother's fiery glint in his eyes.

What is she to write about now, in the silence of this darkened room?

She reads Psalm 119 to her father in the faint light of the

candle, 'Thy word is a lantern unto my feet, and a light to my path.' She watches his familiar face beneath the bandage: the high cheekbones, the decisive nose she has inherited – better on a man than on a woman, she thinks. She stares at the grim mouth, which dips at the corners, the jut of the determined chin, even the fine, broken veins in the cheeks. Her words seem to console and revive him. Blind as he is, smiles play over his face, and joy dawns on his forehead.

She brushes the bristles of white hair, which give him a surprised and unexpectedly roguish air, from his forehead and studies the long oval of his face. She feels a contained elation in the moment, a whisper of self-knowledge. Now that she can be useful to him in his reduced state, she loves him more than ever. She reaches out with the tip of her finger to wipe away a tear, which trickles from his cut left eye, and traces the strong lines of his fine face with her middle finger.

She makes a rough sketch of him in her notebook.

He feels small fingers brush his face like a cobweb. He sniffs at them, at the smell of the body. Since the death of his wife, no one has touched him so. He has almost lost the torment of his celibacy. 'Who is this?' he asks, straining to see. He conjures up his wife's small, neat form, the verbena scent of her skin. 'Maria, is it you?' he says in his dream, and reaches out to catch at her skirts and her slim waist. 'Saucy Pat,' she says, and slaps at his hand.

He sees his wife as she was at the end, begging for relief from pain. All her life she had been so well balanced, so sensible, pious, and self-effacing. Now at the end, the Great Tempter, envying her life of holiness, no doubt, had come to her and disturbed her mind. He sees her plainly, sitting up, her long hair wild about her shoulders, her face pinched and grey, wasted with illness and repellent to him. In her creased gown she reaches out to him, imploring him to help her. 'Where is your damned God now? Where is He?' she screams at him, her hands to her belly where the pain is eating away at her.

Now, for the first time, he understands what she must have felt during those seven long months she lay dying. Then, he could only warn her that blasphemy was a mortal sin and urge her to think of the Judgement to come. 'Help me! Your words are not helping me,' he still hears her scream. He would like to cry out the same words to his daughter, who is sitting beside him, scratching away with her pencil.

When he carried the children into the room – first the eldest, the most pious and brilliant, his favourite, his wife's namesake, and then her favourite, their only boy – thinking it might comfort her to hold them in her arms, she cried out as though he had affronted her. Only the old servant, with her prosaic gestures, was able to calm her. Maria watched her clean the hearth, the way it was done in Cornwall, or let her softly brush her hair or bring a pillow to lift up her legs. Above all, she brought her the laudanum she craved in increasing quantities. 'Give it to me! Give it to me!' she would say, reaching for it. 'This is more help to me than your God.'

In the early afternoon when she lies down to rest and the nurse has gone downstairs for her dinner, Charlotte leaves the door open so she can hear her father's call. She thinks of him lying immobile in the muted light. She thinks of her two living sisters, back home with their burden, their brother, who is probably drinking or drugging himself into a stupor or fit.

She takes out the letter of rejection she keeps in her pocket and rereads the curt words. Her novel, *The Professor*, together with her two sisters' first novels, has come back addressed to the Messrs Currer, Ellis, and Acton Bell, the pseudonyms they have chosen to hide their sex. How much of this triple rejection is due to her sisters' work? She has had her doubts about Emily's, which seems too sombre to her. But Emily would not listen to her counsel. As for Anne's, it is certainly an honest book, but lacks perhaps the force necessary to engage an editor.

The letter had arrived on the day of the operation and came to her as a shock. She was surprised at the intensity, the sharpness, of her feelings. Death almost seemed a way out, but it was driven from her mind as she sat with her father through his ordeal.

How often he has had to still the voice that rises riotously within him. He distinguishes his daughter's light, fast footsteps, her soft voice, her gentle touch, from the nurse's with the hush, hush of her stockings rubbing between her languorous legs, the forced cheer of her voice. He hears them come and go. He drinks in the warmth of his daughter's breath as she leans over him, brushes lightly against his chest, straightens his sheets and blanket. He would like to say: 'Lie down beside me. Warm me with your youth. Warm my dry, old flesh and bones.'

~

She hears her father shouting her name in his sleep. 'Charlotte, Charlotte, Charlotte!' he calls. She rushes to his side in her white gown.

He has shadows like a lace of leaves on his face, a dripping candle burning at his head. He looks grey and cold. She feels the shadow of death upon him. He lies like a stone knight on his back, his hands crossed on his chest. She is afraid he has died, her name on his lips. She approaches with the candle. She cannot hear his breath or see the candle flicker.

She thinks of the story from the Bible of the old king who cannot be warmed until a young virgin is brought to lie beside him. She lies down gently beside him. She stretches an arm above his head. She leans over him to hear his quiet breath.

CHAPTER TWO

Professor

That night, she dreams of her professor, Monsieur H. She is sitting on the white sofa, talking to his wife, yet thinking of him so vividly. He has left on an extended voyage. She pictures the thick, black hair, dark eyes, robust body, wide shoulders, and strong legs. He is dressed casually, without any effort at elegance, in his loose old cloak. She says to his wife, who looks pale and is obviously upset by this long absence, 'You can replace a husband but not a father,' and she sees a small, delicate child standing in the doorway, bent over with grief. The child looks very much like Charlotte herself. She wakes with a start in tears, all her old sorrow returning.

How she had trudged through the damp streets of Brussels, half-crazed with longing, lust, and jealousy, reluctant to return to the school. She lingered there in the dark and the rain to escape black thoughts. She walked to forget her

Master and beloved friend who had replaced her father and her brother – her black swan, the first to discover her talent and encourage her art. How she has waited for his letters!

⁓

It was his wife whom she and Emily met first when they arrived in Brussels that evening, tired and hungry, having somehow lost a suitcase and their way in the dark cobble-stoned streets, which glistened wet in the lamplight. Finally they came to the green door with the bronze plaque in the wall with the name of the *Pensionnat de Demoiselles*. The great door was opened by a small, hunched woman who ushered them inside the bright parlour with its black-and-white marble floor, where they were immediately confronted by a picture of family life that surprised and delighted them. Madame H. was there with her own mother, Madame Parent, as she was called, and sitting close by her side in her old-fashioned dress was Madame Parent's sister. Delicious odours wafted in from the kitchens: baking bread and bubbling stew.

Charlotte and Emily sat side by side on the elegant white sofa so unlike the old dark horsehair one at home. A fat green stove warmed the room. They admired the paintings in their gold frames, the ornaments on the mantelpiece, and the folding doors, which led into the *petit salon* with its piano and enormous draped window.

As they ate something heavy but delicious in a brown sauce with fresh bread followed by an apple tart, Madame Parent regaled them with an exciting tale. She had very blue eyes and a small mouth, and maintained she had been a beauty in her youth. She was a good storyteller and seemed delighted to have new listeners. Though Charlotte was not certain of the truth of her story, she was immediately drawn into it. She had fallen in love with a man who had escaped to Brussels penniless, with the Comte d'Artois, the king's brother, during the French Revolution. The old lady told them her husband had been an elegant man, her eyes glistening and a tremor in her voice, who continued to powder his hair, wear knee breeches, and use the formal *vous* when addressing her.

His sister, she said, a nun of both courage and generosity, had left her convent with a friend, both of them disguised as men. They, also arrived in Brussels, were the ones who had founded this school, which her niece – and here she smiled proudly down at her daughter – now continued to run.

Charlotte, too, admired the ebony-haired and dignified Madame H., a woman in her late thirties who sat very upright, her lace collar perfectly flat. What a relief to be in the company of these hospitable women!

But how unlike them was Monsieur H., a rude and choleric man. The only jarring note in the scene of harmony and family *entente* was his sudden entrance and exit. He came into the black-and-white-tiled hall of the house on the rue d'Isabelle in a cloud of cigar smoke. He was obviously in a hurry, had apparently lost something, and seemed in bad humour. Charlotte watched him open a desk lid and rummage about inside, muttering and sputtering under his breath.

Still, there was something familiar about him. He was like a caricature of a man entering and rummaging about in a desk in a hallway, looking cross. Perhaps she had read such a scene in a book?

Madame H. called to him through the open glass doors of the salon, 'Come, Constantin, dear, and meet our new pupils.' He lifted his head, gave her a stern glance, and strode impatiently into the elegant sitting room.

A small, spare, bespectacled man, he entered with a preoccupied air. With his black hair closely cropped, his brow broad and sallow, and his nostrils wide and quivering, Charlotte decided he looked like a beetle. He seemed to her in a childish rage.

Charlotte pitied Madame H., who appeared to be somewhat older than he, though neither of them was yet in their forties. She remembers thinking, *What an intensely disagreeable and ugly man*, as he bent briefly over her hand with her sister at her side. He hardly took the time to mutter a greeting to his new pupils. Indeed, he seemed to scowl at her particularly and take an instant dislike to both of them.

Madame H. arose to show the sisters to their dormitory. As they walked through the rooms, Charlotte admired the large school buildings. She stopped a moment before the image of the Virgin in an alcove with a burning lamp at her feet and found a prayer rising to her lips: *God give me the courage to live here and do my duty*.

In the dormitory, they were placed at the end of the long row of beds, with extra bed space and a washstand between the beds, providing welcome privacy, and spotless white curtains, which lifted in the breeze.

❧

The next morning they were able to see that the windows overlooked a romantic garden, a haven of quiet and calm in the midst of the city, which would become what she loved more than anything else. She liked to stroll there in the birdsong of early spring mornings or in the calm of the evening, within the shadows of its high walls, its row of pear trees, and its widespread acacia with the fine, feathery leaves, which trembled in the slightest breeze. It made her think of their childhood's imaginary country, Angria, and long for her brother as he had once been. She would have liked to walk with him within such a sheltered garden as this, with its bright blooms, its gravelled walks, and its romantic bower nestled in vines.

From the start, in those first few February days, she admired the orderly but generous way Madame H. ran her school: the young girls were not starved or overworked or obliged to walk to church in wet boots, as Charlotte had once been. Lessons were at reasonable hours: from nine to twelve and then again in the afternoon from two until four. The excellent food they had eaten that first evening proved to be a sample of what was to come. No burned porridge here. Exercise, too, was provided: fresh air in the garden. *Mens sana in corpore sano.*

Or so she thought at first.

She saw him the next morning in the large, sunny classroom where they took their lessons. He taught literature at his wife's school and also at the one for boys next door. From the moment he entered the classroom, he seemed transformed. The dark beetle had become a black swan, the rarest of birds. Monsieur H. sailed in fast, wings spread, obviously in an altered, expansive mood. He was already talking fast, moving his hands furiously through the bright air, as though he were on urgent business. Now, as he mounted the platform, she noticed the broad chest, the strength of the legs, the smiling mouth, the intensity of the black eyes.

He commanded his pupils to sit up and listen. '*Écoutez*,' he trumpeted with authority, and his gaze roamed the room fiercely, searching for an inattentive gaze. He was obviously enjoying himself, the admiring looks of this crowd of young women. When he had their complete attention, he proceeded to read from Racine's *Phèdre* in a fine, deep, resonant voice. He rendered Hippolyte's lines with such feeling and so much expression that, despite her limited French, she forgot where she was, swept away. When he came to a breathless halt and looked around the classroom and the silent, awestruck pupils, she thought, *I am falling in love, falling in love with language, with these sensuous words.*

She listened to him as he analyzed what he had read, probing and darting with daring and eloquence. Despite her limited understanding of the language, she was immediately aware of this man's original mind, his deep comprehension of the many layers of the difficult text. She watched him use all his enthusiasm, his strength of mind and body, to claim the attention, and the hearts and minds, of these young women. Suddenly, she became aware, her mouth was open and her breathing shallow.

Then he handed back the girls' homework, his pupils coming up to claim their work. She saw his expression change again and again, withering one pupil with the movement of lip or nostril and elevating the next with the upturn of an eyebrow. Some wept; others beamed, their faces lit with delight. Sometimes he would produce a little gift for a favourite student who had pleased him particularly, bringing forth something, a bonbon or *gourmandise* from one of his numerous pockets, like a conjuror from a hat.

She knew she wanted to please this man, to see his expression alter, to delight his eyes. She wanted one of his sweet gifts.

CHAPTER THREE

❧

Glimmerings

*H*er father stirs beside her. He gropes in his darkness, and she arrests his wandering hand and imprisons it in both of hers.

'Read me something, dear child, will you? You are my vision. God bless you, child, and reward you,' he says. Gone is the old autocratic tone, the aggravation barely concealed beneath the pious Christian pronouncements, the threats of punishment for sins.

Sitting by her blinded, silenced father, she dares to take up her pencil and write for the first time in her own voice. She writes from experience, using what she knows of life, of literature, of love, plunging into the midst of her tale, not wasting the reader's time or trying her patience with lengthy preliminaries.

This time, she will not hide behind the persona of a man, as she did in her novel *The Professor*, with its two brothers in conflict, or as her younger sister has at the start of her book: no Crimsworth, no Lockwood. Nor will she use the Byronic heroes from her early works: no Wellesley, no Townshend, and above all, no Chief Genius Branii, to tell his tale of war, blood, mire, death, and disaster.

She remembers the direct, engaging voice of Robinson Crusoe – indeed, she feels like Robinson Crusoe, abandoned on her desert island – and she writes as though recounting her own adventures. 'An autobiography,' she writes at the top of the page. She will make them think this is the truth, and it will be.

In their rejection letter, the editors have asked for an exceptional incident. She will give them one – no: many of them. She will give them mystery. She will use compression and little explanation, plunging into action. Above all, no grumbling. She will write out of rage at injustice and arrogance, the religious humbugs, the exploiters.

She works on the first scene, writing rapidly, seeing it all vividly, the shadowy picture emerging fast from the darkness of her mind, this shadowy room: the rainy, grey November day, the aunt's bitter words to the child. 'She regretted to be under the necessity of keeping me at a distance,' the aunt tells the child, her darlings clustered around her before the fire.

This new story of an orphan develops with a kind of urgency she has never known before. She has read and written so much, from such a young age. She knows the child's position in this alien family will yield a steady stream of pathos. She knows how to create suspense by putting a fragile creature in immediate jeopardy and by making her fight back with spirit and justice. 'What does Bessie say I have done?' she has the child retort to the aunt. Let the editor, the reader, put this down!

She contrasts the plain, ten-year-old girl with her richer, better-looking cousins. She invents a bully, a fourteen-year-old boy, John Reed – drawn from her days as governess – a fat child who gorges himself on cakes and sweetmeats. He has sallow skin and two spoiled sisters. How she has suffered at the expense of spoiled children whose doting parents could find no fault in them! She makes her heroine small for her age, delicate, and, like herself, plain. She conjures up a disapproving aunt, a mercurial servant girl.

Charlotte knows about the structure of stories and novels: her beloved Bunyan, Scott, Byron, the German Romantics, the French novels, the great Thackeray, Dickens, Carlyle. She has listened to her teacher's admonitions to imitate classic works. She remembers the fairy tale, where there is an abandoned child, a Cinderella, the parents absent or dead, the aggressor brought swiftly onto the scene. She knows readers will recognize themselves here, all those who had too many brothers and sisters, who were lost in the midst of the solitude of a large family, as she was – or those who had no family at all. An orphan is not so far from a middle child, a third child, soon to be one of six motherless children, with their remote father shut away in his study, muffled in grief. She will avoid mawkishness by creating the complexity of a real child's mind: this child will be no angel.

She remembers her aunt's preference for the other children. She makes up a child who dares to ask what most would want to ask of the uncomprehending adults around her, had they the courage – a bright, brave, imaginative child, the child she would have liked to be. Like Charlotte now in the sombre room, turning the pages of a familiar book, this child is glad of a quiet moment to study the pictures, the words that both echo the loneliness in her heart and carry her away from her solitary place in this family. She dreams of shadowy realms, frozen wastes, uncharted territories. The child is almost happy.

The desolate day outside, the loneliness of the child within the heart of the family, leads to the reading of the book, the escape into pictures, into a dream world. She creates a moment of hope, a slight pause before violence. Perhaps things will be better for her heroine in her hideout, in her world of dreams. Perhaps things will be better for Charlotte, too, starting this new book, alone with her father at her side. Her spirit lifts.

The name of her character and of her book comes to her casually, as she is busy with other things. She thinks of it as she adjusts her father's blanket and lifts a cup to his lips, as he stirs, mutters something, stretches out a hand.

'Are you really there, my dear?' he asks.

'Of course, Papa,' she says, but she is not really there. She plunges on and on into the silvery depths. She floats through the autumn night and leaves this place behind.

It comes to her out of thin air. She is not sure if she has heard such a name. Was there someone she knew with that name? Does it come from the family arms she once saw in a church, or the river she knows well, the beautiful valley of the Ayre? Or is it a name that comes from air, perhaps, or fire? Fire and ire will be in the book: rage at the world as it is. *Unfair! Unfair!* Ire and eyer: she is the one who now sees in her father's place. She has become the voyeur, the observer. Plain Jane, Emily Jane, her beloved sister's second name, Jane, so close to Joan, brave Joan of Arc, Jane so close to Janet, Jeanette, little Jane. A name that conjures up duty and dullness, childhood and obedience, but also spirit and liberty, a sprite's name, a fairy's name, half spirit, half flesh, light in darkness, truth amid hypocrisy, the name of one who sees: Jane Eyre.

CHAPTER FOUR

❧

Love

Sitting at her father's bedside, she has a vision of her French teacher, Monsieur H. She sees him striding fast into the classroom, waving a paper in his hands with that enthusiasm and certainty in his judgement. He draws himself up, staring at her with his intense gaze. She realizes that the paper he holds is hers. He reads from it in his expressive voice, adjusting his glasses. Will he commend it or heap coals of recrimination on her head?

She has written about Napoleon in the freedom of a language that increasingly belongs to her teacher. It is a language of head and heart, of glitter and gleam, a language that she is distanced from and yet now closer to than any other, because of him, a language of enchantment: French.

He trumpets, '*Écoutez!*' and obtains in an instant the complete attention of a roomful of girls in all their youthful giddiness. 'Now listen to this. Observe the range, the promise here. This is lively writing. Pay attention, girls – you'll hear something different, something rare.'

She is not used to compliments. She feels her cheeks flush with pleasure. He has recognized her gift. Her body spins. The whole classroom, with its blackboard, its wooden desks, and its stolid Belgian pupils, swims around her.

❧

She remembers the vacillating spring weather: bright one day and wet the next. As she walked in the garden, how brightly the beds flowered, how darkly the high wall between the boys' and the girls' school cast its shadow on the grass, how sweetly the sounds of the city came to her, like the constant murmur of the sea. How quickly she and Emily learned French, swallowing it down with great joyous gulps until their Master said one day, '*Voilà le Français gagné!*'

She remembers his wife, lying flushed, happy, and exhausted in her canopied bed, smiling at her, as she hesitated at the door with her bouquet of roses clutched in her hand. She welcomed her into the room, patting the bed to invite her to sit close beside her, to admire the new baby she held in her arms. A rush of tears came into her eyes at the sight of the tiny pink creature.

'Would you like to hold him?' the wife asked, but Charlotte didn't dare.

'Yes, yes,' the new mother had insisted, and thrust the little bundle like an offering into her shaking hands. Would she ever carry a baby within her? She lifted the warm infant and kissed his head, inhaling his scent. With this small, helpless being in her arms, she thought quite peculiarly that she would be willing to do anything, anything, to protect this child, if she was called upon to, if he was dependent on her care.

And her teacher, her Master. He seemed in a feverish state during those early days, rushing from one class to the next in his savage-looking old coat or his old-fashioned slouch hat, arriving sometimes unexpectedly in the early morning as she walked alone in the garden.

'*Mademoiselle est bien matinale*,' he would say, pressing her hand in greeting and offering his arm. They walked together under the blossoming fruit trees, the apple, the pear, and the cherry, strolling among the spring flowers, daffodils, tulips, primroses, and fragrant herbs.

In the dim light of her father's room, she recalls the twilight hour and the fluttering of the young girls in muslin dresses like moths in the gloaming between the shadowy trees. She watched him speak with the girls and realized he was not to them what he was to her.

They talked of many things, speaking in French freely in a way she had done with her brother, but here with new words that had no childhood connotations. As then, so now, she felt free. *I cannot fall in love with him, an older and married man*, she had thought.

Their conversation was of the most innocent, she considers, even now, and yet compelling. They had discussed books, her writing, French literature. Her Master had talked at length of the three unities: place, time, and dramatic action. 'The drama must take place offstage, you see. So much more can be suggested than shown, by mysterious sounds, cries from afar, a laugh in the obscurity of the night. The imagination of the reader can do the work.' He was very strict about imitating the classics.

She dared to argue with him. 'But writing cannot be regulated. It is like the cry of the wind or – some sort of electricity.' He looked at her, smiled, and lifted his hand to her hair in a gesture of response, as though words were not enough. She took his hand and put it, in a gesture of admiration, to her lips.

They talked freely about history – the French Revolution, the English queen – about their own histories: his first wife and baby dying suddenly, tragically. Charlotte spoke of her dead older sisters and her brother's dissolution.

'We have much that is similar in our past. For someone so young, you have suffered a lot. I have the impression we are going to be real friends, *amis pour toujours*,' he said.

She looked up at him and felt he knew her heart.

How his moods altered like the spring weather: the showers following fast on a sunny day, greeting her with his generous smile, speaking love with his dark eyes, pressing her hand, lauding her facility with words, often leaving little gifts in her desk: a small, dew-damp bouquet of wildflowers, a book blooming magically between a dull dictionary and a worn-out grammar, or some little sweet pastry nestled unexpectedly in the lap of a dull assignment.

She had never felt so well. She was full of energy, industry, and life. She enjoyed her French studies, her essays, and even her teaching, which she began to do for Madame H. with trepidation, taking over the role of the English teacher in the classroom with increasing authority, blossoming in the sun of Monsieur H.'s approbation. She realized she, too, could stand before students and hold their attention, share with them the things she knew. She, too, could teach.

One evening, as they stood at twilight under the acacia tree, the sky an orange-pink, as she looked up at him adoringly, all her throbbing heart in her gaze, he had bent down close, pressing his heavy, hard body against her, brushing her cheek with his damp lips, stealing a brief kiss, whispering in her ear. 'Who,' he said. 'Who is my best girl?'

'Your wife,' she had answered, but feebly, her voice shaking. How could he ask such a question? What did it mean?

'If only, if only . . .' And she felt his body swelling with a promise she could only guess at, as he pressed himself against her.

Her existence was filling up in Belgium for a while, as it does now here in Manchester, sitting beside her father, writing this book, which comes to her so fast and clearly. Once again she feels that spring sultriness here, in the close rooms in Manchester, where she keeps the fire going for her father.

CHAPTER FIVE

Writing

Wh at a luxury to be able to sit here hour after hour in the muffled light and the silence of the city! She writes all through the day with little interruption except for her father's few murmured requests and the light food the nurse brings him. She helps herself from his tray. She shares the strained breakfast porridge, the tapioca, familiar food from her childhood. She eats all her meals close beside him. She feeds him. He opens his lips on the spoon like a baby bird. She wipes his lips and chin, and then her own. She hands the tray back to the nurse, a coarse-faced woman who disturbs her work. Then she takes up her pencil again.

The writing is her way out of this room, this cell of solitude, darkness, and despair. Her mind is free to roam where it will. She dares to take up her humiliations and heartaches and to give them a structure. She thinks of the plot like Pilgrim's voyage, a loosely linked chain of events, the battle with one danger leading to the next: causality.

৶৶

As the story takes shape, it lifts her out of the gloom of her failures at life and love. 'What do you want?' the ten-year-old girl asks the bully who finds her in her hideout and disturbs the reading of her favourite book.

Sitting beside her helpless father, she completes the scene. When the boy insults her and throws the precious book at her, she has Jane strike back. 'Wicked and cruel boy!' she says. 'You are like a murderer.' Blood seeping from her head wound, she compares him to the Roman emperors, to Caligula and Nero. She makes active what has been passive in life. Her Jane retaliates with violence, like a bad animal who claws and must be punished; she is carried off to the Red Room. There, despite her protests, she is cruelly abandoned. Her aunt shuts her up entirely alone in the room with its large bedstead, damask curtains, shrouded windows, and looking glass, where her husband, Jane's uncle, breathed his last.

Like her Jane, who sits in the dark on her stool in the locked room, Charlotte has no need for bonds. She feels that if she left her father now he might disappear, as though it is her dim sight that holds him hovering in half life, as though she has invented him and not he her.

Charlotte rises and walks across the darkened room. A pale face she hardly recognizes glimmers back at her from the looking glass, like an illustration in a child's book, a goblin half-emerging from behind a curtain. She sees a small, childlike, neckless, insignificant person with irregular features. *Who is here? What stranger is this?* Why is this person not more like the models she studied as a girl in the annuals? Where is the perfectly oval face, the long, aristocratic neck, the alabaster shoulders, and the swanlike carriage? Above all, she thinks, drawing back her upper lip, where are the even teeth?

So often she slips into a room in the shadows. She hugs the wall. She has the sort of face and figure people compliment, saying she has such expressive eyes, such lovely, light-brown hair, such dainty hands and feet. Or, she has been told, she has a smile that speaks of forbearance, courage, and loyalty.

A paralyzing fear only small children feel, a fear of ghosts and spirits, comes to her again. She thinks of her Methodist aunt's terrible tales of sin and eternal damnation: 'Say your prayers, child, for if you don't repent, something bad might come and fetch you away.' She longs for her mother's protection. At the same time she remembers her mother's last words, which were for her children, and what she feared most was that her dead mother might come back to them in the night to make sure her last wishes were being carried out and her poor children in good hands.

Now the ghosts of all the departed are gathered here at her father's bedside: her mother, her two older sisters, her dear friend, Martha, who died young and far from home. She hears a gust of dry air beating on the windows and a cry in the quiet street below. Candlelight flickers on the ceiling.

How far into this underworld does she dare to go? Will she find her way back?

The ghost of the mother's brother comes to the child, Jane, in the Red Room. The ghost terrifies both her and her creator. Jane cries out in desperation for help.

Charlotte leans over her exercise book now for solace and lifts it to her eyes, which, like her father's, have never been good. She is accustomed to writing this way, but through the haze of tears she cannot read what she has written. She brushes her hand over the page and goes on. The early light, almost as blue as moonlight, filters through the curtains.

CHAPTER SIX

❧

Reality

*I*n the half dark her father imagines he is back in the parlour where he first saw his future wife. He hears the rustling of her skirts and her lively, booted steps as she trips into the room. She stands before him, the light behind her. Plain, erect, correct, in a pale dress, she hovers shyly at her aunt's side. 'How do you do?' she says demurely to him. She bobs a curtsy, and he takes her small, cool hand in his large, hot one. She moves from him, going over to the sideboard and politely offering him lemonade from a glass pitcher. After his long walk in the August heat, he is thirsty. 'I'd appreciate that,' he says, though he would prefer something stronger. He stares at her as she pours, and she glances back. There is something frank and playful in her smile that moves him as she offers him the glass and her cold fingers touch his.

He thinks how his wife's family would have scorned his

poor parents, the Pruntys, from County Down, had he not entered their parlour caparisoned in the sable of the clergy-man, with his degree from Cambridge and his altered name.

He remembers his wife's easy wit, her irreverent sense of fun, her good sense, her strong Methodist faith, and what pleased her 'saucy Pat', as she called him, best of all: her fast-growing infatuation with him. He remembers her lively letters, in which she told him that he was replacing her God for her.

At twenty-nine, his wife was not much younger than this daughter at his side. She must almost have given up hope of marrying, despite her dowry of fifty pounds a year.

He remembers the joyous wedding, her frightened shyness on the wedding night. 'Let us first get to know one another better,' she had said firmly, leaving him breathless beside her, filled with lust, the scent of her skin in the air, the soft sound of her breathing in the dark. The soft sweetness of her body against his, the night when she finally succumbed to him, comes back.

'Perhaps we could wait a few more days,' his wife had said, as he dared to reach for her waist, to draw her firmly to him. She had kept him waiting a long while.

'I have been waiting for years,' he had found the courage to say, half-playfully, half-exultantly, as she lay trembling beside him in her long white nightdress, her frilled nightcap. 'What difference would a few more days make? I am your husband. I have been patient, and you have promised to obey.'

'Tell me what I must do,' she had whispered then. And,

indeed, when he thinks about it now, it was a fearful thing to have done.

Then, young, impatient, and sure of his rights, he had told her. He has almost forgotten the feeling of her tender, shy touch, as he guided her small hand to the place where he throbbed and yearned.

'No, I can't,' she said, drawing back as though he were made of fire. 'Not that.'

'Help me. Then it will be quick,' he promised, and indeed, it was.

He has not forgotten those wild, brief plunges into her small, obedient body, nor the prayers she offered up to her God as he worked fast with quick, brutal thrusts; and the relief she brought him again and again, a relief he came to count on night after breathless night, and one she never denied him, despite the repeated pregnancies, one every year for six years, despite her soft pleas for respite.

'Not yet. I'm not well yet. In a while, please, dear. I am so tired. Another baby would kill me,' she would say.

'A wife's duty,' he had only to remind her for her to open up her body to him. Somehow, strangely, it excited him to think of his wife performing her duty, muttering her prayers: *please God help me, please God help me, please,* while he took his rightful pleasure. He remembers how she would cross herself afterward and say, 'In the name of the Father and the Son and the Holy Ghost, amen.' He remembers the strong odour of her body after sex.

Perhaps, he thinks, if he could have found another wife who would have taken them on, been a real mother to them, they would all have prospered. They cannot say he did not try. But what woman in her right senses would take him and six small children in charge in that remote, cold place on a stipend of two hundred pounds a year?

He thinks of the irony of his solitary cohabitation for so many years with his wife's spinster sister, her fifty pounds a year replacing his wife's fifty. How she hoarded her store. He remembers her five-pound gift for the new church organ and how difficult it was to obtain. He was prohibited by the laws of his Church from taking her as his wife, should he have so desired.

In his near blindness he has become more conscious of sounds: the drip of the candle wax at his head and the hard drumming of his own heart, as though he were young again and racing across a field. Less reassuring are the smells, those of this nurse, with her soap, carbolic acid, garlic breath, and disturbing perfume. At the same time he smells this daughter, whom he holds close beside him now. He detects a scent that reveals an emotion: the faint, slightly stale smell of sadness, something dragged from her pores by anguish. He presumes she will never marry, will never bear children, will remain dutifully at his side through his life, a comfort to him. He senses his daughter has not had a joyful moment since her return from the school in Brussels. He hears her sob softly, smells her perfume of sandalwood and regret. He lifts his hand and gropes to find her hand, feel her face, wipe a tear from her cheek.

He wonders now what happened to her at that school. What took her back to it on her own? Could it have been some deception of the heart? What happened with her French Master, who had written to him so kindly about both his girls, asking them to remain as teachers at the school where they had been pupils? Should he have allowed her to go? Could this good girl have sinned in some way? He knows he has done so himself. His were sins of pride, of intolerance and anger. Is he being punished for his sins? *God forgive me, please! We acknowledge and bewail our manifold sins and wickedness.* He remembers his fury at the bell ringers who had dared to practise their craft on the Sabbath; how he had charged at them waving his *shillelagh* in the air over his head, shouting about the Sabbath. But hers?

What is she writing? A letter to her sisters? A poem? Some melodramatic tale? At this hour of the night? What could she have to say? What does she know about the world?

The words of the Scriptures come to him: *Regard the lilies of the fields they sew not neither do they spin, yet, I say unto you, even Solomon in all his glory was not arrayed in such glory as these.*

He asks her, 'Do you remember how fiercely you and Branwell would quarrel over Wellington's and Buonaparte's relative merits?'

She says nothing, and the sound of her scribbling continues anew and gratingly.

'Do you ever hear from your professor, your French Master?' he whispers into the dark. She answers not at all, and continues her scribbling.

'What is it, dear?' he asks. 'Is there something amiss?' But still she does not respond. He feels her move away.

He would like so much to say something to comfort her, lift this burden of sadness from her shoulders, as he would have liked to help his dying wife. The truth is, he realizes, he still doesn't know the right words.

He shifts his weight on the bed. He says, 'At least I gave you that time in Brussels, first with Emily and then alone.'

Does he know what he is saying? she wonders. Does he remember how they paid for the journey themselves with their aunt's gift? She knows how difficult it has always been for him to let them go.

CHAPTER SEVEN

Jealousy

A letter arrived at the school in Brussels one afternoon after tea, telling of her aunt's illness. She and Emily would have to return to Haworth immediately. She had no choice. She would have to leave her Master.

They arrived at the parsonage only to find her aunt already dead. She remembers the dull days that followed, her beloved home now a desert to her, and her longing to return to Brussels. Then her Master's kind letter arrived, summoning them back, offering employment as teachers. She remembers her elation on her return to the school, alone, leaving Emily behind with her father.

She had given her Master English lessons. She had become his *maître* or rather his *maîtresse* in the schoolroom. She had scolded him! How she had laughed at his accent! What pleasure she had in being in charge of him, in the reversal of roles, just as she enjoys it now in this dark room with her helpless father.

Suddenly, he had broken off the English lessons. 'I have too much to do,' he had said, not looking her in the eye. 'We cannot be selfish. You must devote your time to others, not to me. You are too exclusive. Make friends with some of the other teachers, or even the girls. It would be good for them and for you,' and he hurried from the room.

How could he expect her to make friends with the other teachers – all silly, superficial women without gifts! Surely he knew that. They had often laughed together over them. As for the students, they were unworthy of her interest, stolid and vain. In each of them she saw nothing but false sentiment, stupidity. How could he suddenly expect her to take an interest in them? She was furious. Yet she could not stop watching him.

At moments he looked so young in a belted blouse and cheerful hat, surrounded by his gaggle of girls. Was his colourless face, the massive brow and dark eyebrows, without charm? Did she stare at him and take pleasure in the staring? Was it such a pleasure as a thirsty man feels at drinking a glass of fresh water in a desert? Did he still seem ugly to her? No, no, reader, he did not, he did not at all; just as her father lying beside her still impresses her with his white hair, his dignity, and courage. She breathes softly on his forehead, flutters his hair, and he mutters her name.

But her black swan hardly seemed to notice her, though she had come back from Haworth because of him, with the hope of sharing her work with him. She had brought her writing with her, her precious Angrian chronicles, which she had dared to show him.

Often now he ignored her or even berated her. He would scowl and stamp his small, booted foot. 'How could you write something of the sort!' He accused her of melodrama, of a ridiculous romanticism. 'What about the three unities?' he asked her. 'What about understatement? What about control!'

After several days of coldness and unbearable silence, of scowls and scorn, she had seen him rushing down the pergola, which ran along the edge of the garden. It was an early spring morning. A breeze blew his cloak about his legs and the dust up in the air. She had caught up with him, clutched onto his arm, drawn him close, looked into his eyes. She had so much wanted to cry out, 'I must talk to you. You cannot treat me thus – Do you think I don't feel what other people do, that I don't long for the same things as you! I cannot bear your silence, your coldness, your inhumanity! I cannot live without a kind word from you. Did you not say we would be friends, friends *pour toujours*! How can I forget what has happened between us? Is that too much to ask of you? A moment of friendship? A kind word?' But she knew they were words she would immediately regret, words a woman could not afford to use with a man, let alone a married one. She had just stood there wordlessly, biting her lip, tears in her downcast eyes.

Monsieur H. had drawn himself up and looked over his shoulders to see if anyone was nearby. There was a smell of dust, honeysuckle, and lilac in the air. 'What is it?' he had hissed impatiently, freeing himself from her grasp, dusting himself off, as though she were dust, as though her grasp had soiled him.

'What is the matter with you?' he said, and when she could not speak, the tears falling silently down her cheeks, 'For goodness' sake, Mademoiselle, control yourself! Above all, self-control.'

What had hurt most was her sense that this scene, or some aspect of her behaviour, had been reported to the wife. She had been discussed. Perhaps this was not the first time something of this kind had occurred with an overly enthusiastic student. She had imagined the couple lying quietly side by side that night in their bed, a splendid spring night, the windows open on the garden, all the night odours of sweet-briar and southernwood, of jasmine, and early-blooming roses in the air. She saw him lying with his wife's hand on his arm, her warm, milk-full breasts half-exposed in her pink peignoir, her raven locks loose and glossy. She was nestling against his wide chest, while another new baby, a little girl this time – how rapidly and easily the woman produced them, an endless supply – slept sweetly in the cot at the foot of the bed. She could hear the little snuffling breath.

'I can see something is wrong. Something is bothering you. Is it some student? Some awkwardness with one of the girls?' Charlotte sees the wife push the thick hair back from his forehead, caress his square forehead and dark brows gently, letting her hand linger on his chest. She presses her breasts against his side, entwines her legs with his. She sighs and adds, 'You know I can always help you when it is necessary, my darling,' and shifts her hips closer to his.

Then he sighs, closes his book with a snap, turns to her, and repeats that it is nothing really – *un rien du tout*. Though his voice wavers, and though he tells her otherwise, she has already won.

'Nothing at all? Are we so sure?' she says half-playfully, wagging a finger while she leans her warm body against him. And then he confesses. It all comes out confusedly.

There is, indeed, a student who has some sort of silly crush on him, once again.

'Who is it, my dear?'

He hesitates an instant, but she looks at him inquiringly, and he admits, 'One of the two English sisters, the elder one – a lonely, plain girl.'

'I suspected something of the sort,' she says. 'That girl is too ambitious. I could see that. She needs to be put in her rightful place.'

'Why does this happen to me?' he asks in all innocence, shrugging and waving his hands in the air as he does in the classroom.

'It's because you're too good, Constantin, my dear, I keep telling you. You give too much of yourself in the classroom. You should never have consented to read that girl's work, to encourage her. A mistake I warned you against, you will remember.' And Charlotte hears her add, in her practical Belgian way, 'Don't worry; I'll take care of it. All you have to do is to promise me to ignore the girl completely.'

'How can I do that? She is my student, a paying student, after all.'

'Not paying that much at this point – we are paying her

46

for her teaching. She gets her room and board free, after all. She only pays for her laundry. You can treat her with polite coldness – nothing more. Promise me, will you?' and she looks him in the eye.

'Of course, of course, my dear.'

He had kept his word.

After that, his wife took things into her capable Belgian hands. She watched Charlotte's every movement, set her spy on her – the other young French teacher – a vain, superficial woman who was, no doubt, in her pay. She saw the two of them whispering together, sharing information about her, surely. Perhaps Madame H. spied herself, shuffling surreptitiously along the hallways like the ladies at the French court, in her soft, silent Belgian slippers, her dark clothes, appearing suddenly without warning, her face wreathed in false smiles, her mouth in caressing words.

Charlotte was certain someone had foraged in her intimate things, hunted through her underclothes, found the pressed flower he had given her between the leaves of her book and replaced it between other pages, even read her few precious letters from home. How dared she touch her most cherished letters! She could smell the wife's, or perhaps it was the French teacher's, cloying perfume in her things, while all the while the wife maintained a polite, even amiable front. How she came to hate her, her falseness, her hypocrisy, her *sournoiserie*. How could he have married her?

Now her teacher moved away whenever she came near, turned his back on her and rushed down the stairs, as though she had a contagious disease.

Madame H. had sought her out and attempted to extract a confession from her. 'You seem a little sad, a little pale, my dear. I do hope nothing is wrong. Is there anything we can do? You must come and sit with me in the evening like this in our sitting room if you feel lonely. I know what loneliness is like, and homesickness, or a little trouble of the heart, perhaps?' She stroked the white sofa where she and Emily had sat with such delight that first evening at the school. Now she leaned so near that Charlotte could feel the soft contour of her breast brush against her and smell the cloying, nauseating perfume.

Charlotte wondered what other functions she served in this woman's marriage? She was tempted to speak her mind as she sat by the wife. She watched her sew in the sitting room, where she knew Monsieur H. had sat, where she could still smell the lingering odour of his cigar, where she might even still hope to catch a glimpse of him. She was tempted to unburden herself to this woman who was surely his confidante. She wanted to shout at her: *I know you hate me, stop pretending! How can you be such a hypocrite? I know you are jealous of me, of your husband's attention to me. You are jealous of my work, my writing, my gift, which he has recognized. I know you would like to keep me teaching forever, paying me a pittance for my hard work!* But she knew to keep quiet, as now she denies any trouble to her father when he asks her, 'Charlotte, dear, is anything troubling you?'

'Just a headache, a little fatigue,' she says. She lies badly, as she did in Brussels, knowing she would suffer even more if she did speak, like a child drawn to a bakery window, standing outside and staring with longing at the sight of the plump, warm, and redolent bread.

With the school emptied for the summer, the H.'s gone to the seaside, the empty halls and dormitories rang with the hollow sound of her steps. She sat through those long, bright, silent hours and felt she could not have been more desolate if she had been abandoned in the wastes of the Sahara without water or food. Sometimes she felt she would not be able to bear the solitude. Her busy brain worked restlessly, and her thoughts returned ceaselessly to him. *Please, God, let him think of me. Let him come to me!* She had so few things to think about, and he had so many! While she thought of him at every moment, she imagined him surrounded by his family, his wife, his friends, his mind on other things. *Unfair! Unfair!*

Every detail of the old school is imprinted indelibly on her mind as she sits quietly beside her father's bedside writing in the half dark about Jane. Charlotte sees the Madonna in the alcove, the flowers at her feet, where she found herself whispering desperate prayers; the white bed hangings that swayed in the sultry summer air; the garden above all in the moonlight as the honeydew fell and the gloaming gathered, with its flowering parterres and fruit trees and the smell of his cigar that lingered and which she breathed in rapturously.

She was certain she smelled it one autumn morning when school had resumed. She lifted the lid of the desk, already scenting the precious odour. She imagined his hand lifting up the desk, rummaging freely yet gently, fingering her things. For there, among the books and pencils, her *cahiers*, she found the welcome traces of his presence, signs and stains he had left behind, the order of things altered, a nib dipped into ink, a pencil sharpened. There she found the book in German he had left her, signed for her on its flyleaf. He had thought of her. He had not forgotten her completely. He had dared to disobey his wife. How her heart lifted up with joy, the whole classroom, filled with the dull girls, suddenly bright and shining. She was obliged to step into the garden for a moment, to draw breath.

She kept hoping he would come to her. She lingered there in the early mornings, staring at the leaves, the shrubs, the birds, or late at night, gazing up at the stars, longing to see something more, the dark shadow of a human figure of a certain mould and height. She could not bring herself to leave, to move on. She was stalled.

All of this comes back to her in Manchester. This is the time in her life when she writes hour after hour, day after day. She realizes the working conditions are the most perfect she will ever find: silence in company, perpetual night. These rooms in this strange town allow her to write freely, but they will soon be lost to her. As soon as her father begins to recover, she will take him back to her sisters, her brother, Haworth. She must hurry.

CHAPTER EIGHT

❧

Nurse

What the nurse worries about, as she sits by the old man's side with her sewing, is the provisions. She is feeling peckish but smells no reassuring morning aromas: no rashers or sausage frying. She could do with something substantial for her breakfast. She imagines a nice kipper, a soft poached egg, black pudding, or even a bit of bread, fried in the drippings, but is afraid there will be only Scottish oatmeal again, and that not in great quantity.

She wonders if they have ordered sufficient amounts. She doubts the old servant provided by the doctor will serve up enough food. Last night's dinner was a disaster: some sort of cod served almost cold in a watery, white sauce and sprinkled with a few capers. Do these people realize how much food will be necessary for their sojourn together over several weeks? she thinks, watching the daughter enter the room and take up her seat in the alcove with her notebook.

The daughter seems inexperienced, or certainly betrays a lamentable disinterest in the managing of household matters, things that any woman should surely be familiar with. When she attempted to give her certain excellent recipes, she had been ignored. Yet she is no slip of a girl. What is wrong with her? She spends her whole day with her nose in that notebook. There are three of them, after all – four, counting Biddy, the servant – and they have not ordered much meat or poultry. She does not relish the thought of eating potatoes and porridge for the next five weeks. She has a hearty appetite and as well as her kipper for breakfast or even a bit of steak and kidney pie, she likes a juicy mutton chop with a mushroom for her dinner and a pint of porter to accompany it. She considers a certain amount of meat and poultry necessary for the work she has to accomplish. In the daughter's place she would have lain on a loin of lamb, cooked in advance, a couple of pig's trotters, and a few mince pies in the larder.

She lifts a cup of tea to her patient's dry lips, and he sips it. She says, 'A little broth, perhaps?' and spoons some of the tasteless stuff between her poor patient's lips. The nurse wishes she could leave this small, shabby house, these silent people, and go to her three little girls. She would like to hug them, swing them around in the air, hear them laugh. She thinks of her husband, a bricklayer, who was killed in a fall from a stepladder two years before. She remembers the sweet taste of his mouth.

Her patient nibbles at the piece of bread and butter she offers up to him, but after the first taste refuses the sliver of cold mutton. Almost gagging, he pushes away the offered food impatiently. She rebukes him for his recalcitrance.

'But you must keep up your strength, Reverend.'

⤳

She slips the pan beneath the blanket, where his skinny, old-man shanks lie. She waits by the door, turning her gaze away. No doubt he feels her presence, waiting, but now, apparently, the urge has disappeared. Nothing seems to be happening. She is used to this. She remains where she is while he strains to produce a small offering for her, to take advantage of this opportunity she has given him. She hears a slight rustle and drop. She goes over to the bed, catching a glimpse of his body as she lifts the blanket to reclaim the pan. He lies stiffly on the enamel, shivering, his worm of a member drooping between his legs. She wipes him clean and removes the pan.

Will she be exposed to such helpless humiliation in her old age? Will she, too, be deprived of the most elemental dignity, like this old man? It reminds her of her early dreams of nakedness, of being stripped of her clothes in a public place. The thought is horrifying now, but perhaps she will not mind by then. She remembers how she felt when her babies were born. She did not care who saw her naked or even what happened at that moment to the baby, the little tadpole swimming its way into life.

⤳

There are these narrow stairs she must negotiate. Up and down, up and down, several times a day, bedpan in hand, she risks breaking her neck. Her boots pummel the floorboards. She presumes they will need her to stay for the five or six weeks the old man will have to lie here, flat on his back. Or so Dr Wilson has told her.

The nurse is not sure how long she will want to stay on here, whether or not the food is sufficient. She walks across the small back garden, a few zinnias strangled in their dry beds, a dusty chestnut tree, thin cypresses against a wall. She looks up into the leaves. The edges are brown. She feels a shift in the weather, the sun obscured by cloud. Trapped heat rises from the earth. The privy is at some distance from the main building, at the back of the narrow house. The nurse empties the pan and then relieves herself while she is at it, sitting for a moment despite the strong smell and contemplating her solid black boots, listening to the buzzing of a trapped fly, a moment of repose.

Back in the garden, a light breeze blows the ribbons from her cap about her plump arms, and the thin cypresses sway. She enters the dark, redbrick building and glances into the dingy, ground-floor kitchen. She nods good-day to Biddy, who seems rather deaf and uncommunicative and is peeling potatoes over the sink. Her work is not difficult, she will admit, as Dr Wilson has promised, and the parson is a quiet, uncomplaining patient, but there is always the danger of infection in such cases. She is a great believer in the efficacy of leeches. She must suggest this to the doctor when he calls later today.

What the doctor has not foreseen is that living in close proximity, day after day, with these two does not appeal to her. She climbs the stairs and reenters the darkened room. For a moment it looks as if her patient has disappeared. Then she sees him, lying patiently on his back in the shadows, his daughter dutifully at his side in her bilious, dark-green dress.

The scant provisions are not the only signs of hardship. The daughter's dress – with the old-fashioned *gigot* sleeves, the grey fichu, the petticoats without a flounce or a wave, the way the dress hangs on her body, though neat enough – looks out of date and dowdy, after all, to one who has worked for some of the better families in Manchester. These two may not realize it, but she has been in some demand. She can pick and choose her cases. Nursing work may not be distinguished, but there is no shortage of it for the young, strong, competent, and, if she says so herself, attractive.

The silence in the room weighs on her, as she bustles around, straightening things up. The daughter goes on scribbling in her book without lifting her head. *What would a spinster like her have to say?* The old man lies so still, he might be dead. He takes his lot with grim resignation and has been told not to talk or move, of course. But the daughter puts on unnecessary airs, hardly saying a word or, when she does utter a few, muttering them almost incomprehensibly and in such a soft, doleful voice she can hardly be heard. The daughter appears almost as blind as the father, as she lifts the book up to her nose or bends down low to it.

She wonders if she should say something about the scant provisions. The daughter looks up, as if she senses this thought, and even in the dim light the nurse sees a momentary flash, a spark of smouldering fire in the large, luminous eyes behind the glasses, which surprises her. *Perhaps not as mild and meek as one might think at first glance.*

The daughter turns from her immediately and plunges her nose back into her writing book. *Who do you think you are, dearie?* She is accustomed to a bit of a bustle, a friendly word now and then, an appraising glance, even from the most aristocratic of her patients.

When she worked for Lady Sedick last summer at Thornton, there were the housekeeper who chatted with her at length in her cosy sitting room in the evenings and the groom, who had his eye on her. She can still see him as he was early that spring morning when she took a turn in the dew-wet garden: a big, sandy-haired, strapping young fellow, standing astraddle in the sunlight in his mire-flecked boots, offering her a big bowl of wild strawberries he had picked from the garden, swimming in cream. Irresistible.

Even Lady Sedick, herself, whose husband was absent most of the time, liked to converse about her ailments at some length, particularly in the middle of the night when she could not sleep. She would call her at moments like that, plaintively, and ask her to bring her a *tisane* and perhaps a little biscuit. She would dip the biscuit into her cup and wet her lips, the dark hair on the upper lip damp. Sometimes she would even hold her hand or have her brush out her thin hair. 'My dear, my dear, if you knew how I suffer,' she would say, and press her hand to her heart. Sometimes, when she had asked her to massage her shoulders and back, and if the nurse would allow the tips of her trembling fingers just to touch her décolleté with delicacy, she would make a little moaning sound and say, 'What healing hands you have, my dear.'

-ℓℓ-

She wakes in the night, unable to sleep. 'Forgive me, God. Just to let me sleep,' she whispers, and places her hand between her thighs, strokes gently, crosses her legs on her hand. She groans with relief. Still, she does not fall asleep. She needs something more solid in her stomach than the watery fish they had again for dinner. She would like a piece of cheese, a little of the lamb left over from the day before.

She climbs out of her bed, pulls a shawl over her shoulders, and barefooted, candle in hand, creeps quietly down the stairs. She goes into the basement kitchen and takes the lamb bone from its dish in a cupboard, pours herself a pint of porter, and sits down at the table. She takes the bone in both hands and gnaws at it, ravenously. Nothing quite as delicious as the flesh near the bone. She is grinding on a delicious piece of gristle with her good back teeth when the kitchen door swings open and someone stands staring at her, a flash of surprise in her eyes. It is the daughter in her white nightgown, her hair around her shoulders.

'What are you doing here?' she asks, though it is perfectly obvious.

'I couldn't sleep,' she says, embarrassed, dropping the bone, springing to her feet, wishing she had put on shoes. She wipes the grease from her chin with the back of her hand and lowers her gaze like a guilty child.

The daughter looks at her for a moment and then smiles. 'Neither could I,' she says, not unkindly.

'Would you like something to eat – drink?' the nurse asks, gathering her wits about her.

The daughter hesitates, eyeing the lamb bone and the porter. There is a flash of greed in her eye.

The nurse pours her a generous glass of porter, and the daughter makes a gesture to her to sit down. They sit facing each other across the kitchen table in the night silence, sipping. She can see the traces of the porter in the fine hairs on the daughter's upper lip. *What a small, dainty woman!*

'Such long, lonely nights,' the daughter says, and in the soft light, her pretty hair down, her eyes bright, the nurse finds herself thinking she looks almost beautiful.

CHAPTER NINE

❦

Hope

Charlotte, too, has had difficulty sleeping. She has heard footsteps on the stairs. She has gone down to see who was roaming around. She found the nurse sitting before a candle on her own in the kitchen, her shawl around her shoulders, chomping on the lamb bone left from dinner, grease shining on her broad cheeks, blunt chin, and wide mouth, her big, bare feet splayed on the kitchen floor. She had wanted to giggle with her like a naughty schoolgirl. She had drunk a whole glass of porter and even climbed the stairs with her, taken her hand, and wished her a good night.

She has found an imaginary name for her: Humber.

She is goaded on by the letter in her pocket, containing the rejection that had come on the morning of her father's operation from the publisher who had turned down their three volumes; and by the poor sales of her poems and her sisters'. She is still convinced of the merit of Emily's poetry, though little good has come of it as yet. *The moor-lark in the air / The bee among the heather-bell.* The line with its precise details, its hidden rhythms, still makes her shiver slightly. Surely it will remain? They have had to pay for the publication themselves, and so far only two volumes of 165 pages have been sold, at four shillings each.

She is determined not to write any more pathetic, begging letters to her professor, her Master, and to stop thinking about him, other than to use him in her work, the ultimate revenge. She has given up all hope for her once-beloved brother. Her disillusionment with him is now complete and commensurate with her former adulation. Their physical similarity, their susceptibility to passion, make her determined to detach herself from him. She will transform these fallible creatures into objects that will serve her purposes. She will use all those who have snubbed and ignored her. She will write out of rage, out of a deep sense of her own worth and of the injustice of the world's reception of her words. She will write about something she knows well: her passion.

She has the habit of writing with her eyes closed, shutting out the world. There is no need for this. She has written so many words in her short life, many of them with her brother. They were two beings with one sensibility, one imagination, their nerves vibrating to the same chords. Was that but practice for this moment?

She would like to reach other women, large numbers of them. She would like to entertain, to startle, to give voice to what they hold in secret in their hearts, to allow them to feel they are part of a larger community of sufferers. She would like to show them all that a woman feels: the boredom of a life confined to tedious domestic tasks. Perhaps she can reach even this nurse, with her busy beneficence, whose quack-quack voice and loud laugh grate upon her ears, who bustles around them so officiously and feeds her face.

Charlotte dozes and wakes in her chair, and for a moment is not sure where she is. She becomes aware of a red glow in the room from the low fire in the fireplace. Of course: she is in Manchester. A stranger stands before her. She rises quickly to her feet and adjusts the lace collar of her dress. 'I must have dozed,' she says.

The doctor, for it is he, gives her his hand. Not a tall man, he has a sharp, narrow, but kindly face; large, deep-set eyes; thick, wavy white hair. The nurse, who has retreated to the other room, has ushered him in. He goes to her father's bedside, a comforting presence as he stands there, bending over, his bright head a white glimmer of light like a halo over her father, speaking softly to him. She watches him in the candlelight as he removes the bandage carefully, lifts the eyelid. His slender, well-kept hands hold her attention – quick, active, and unconstrained hands. She approaches and looks down at her father's eyes, which seem to stare back at her. Can he see her?

'Do you see anything?' the doctor asks.

'I see something dimly, as through a glass darkly,' her father says.

'Ah! and can you make out any object, or any light?' the doctor asks.

'I can see a glow – a ruddy haze,' he says, looking in the direction of the fire.

'And the candlelight?' he asks.

'A luminous cloud,' her father says.

The doctor pronounces himself entirely satisfied with the results of the operation. In her enthusiasm Charlotte reaches out her hand. He takes it first in one, then in both of his. 'Oh, thank you,' she says. 'You have saved our . . .' but she is unable to finish her sentence, the thrill of his healing hands running all through her body like warm water.

At the same time an idea comes to her for her book. Moments of hope will come to Jane with the kind apothecary's words. Perhaps Jane will leave her aunt and cousins, the Reeds' house, her unkind relatives, and go away to school.

Charlotte would so like to detain the doctor, to put her head on his shoulder, to lean against him. She imagines saying, *Do stay and take tea with us*, offering him tarts, buttered crumpets, strawberry jam, seed-cake, though they have not, of course, ordered such delicacies. But he is in a hurry, he says; there are other patients to visit, he explains, and he is too soon gone. Her moment of exhilaration disappears.

CHAPTER TEN

✤

Awakening

*T*he nurse folds back his blanket but leaves the sheet over his old, stiff body. She takes out first a hand, then an arm, and then a leg, without looking. She wipes his skin carefully with a warm, damp cloth, so as not to move his head. She sees how he unclenches his fists, lets himself go.

She murmurs, 'Lie very still,' as she uncovers his chest. 'You will hardly feel this.'

He is suddenly glad to be lying here resting in silence, his sight gradually healing, forms and faint light flickering. A calm falls on him like gentle and consoling rain. *My prayers have been answered. Thanks be to God.* He lies still, still, obedient in this woman's competent hands. *What a blessing not to have to go anywhere or listen to anyone, not to have to comfort, to search for soothing words, not to have to reassure with false hope or help with brave words or actions.*

As far back as he can remember, he has worked. As a boy

in the fields, he worked with his hands; later he worked with his mind. He sees himself as a small boy, sitting in the hut, with the mud floor, the whitewashed walls, the one small window, the visible thatched roof with its beams exposed, and the odour of roasting corn in the air. Everyone else sleeps heavily, while he bends over the rough table, straining his eyes on the fine print of the family Bible. He is reading it from cover to cover, learning word after beautiful word by heart, even the dull 'begat' chapters. Despite his exhaustion, the aching of his limbs after a day in the fields, his hunger for food, he is desperate to acquire the learning that will allow him to advance in the world so that he can become a gentleman.

There were few books beside the Bible, Milton, and Bunyan's *Pilgrim's Progress* in their house. His mother had no time for them. He was obliged to help his father in the fields or to care for the many young ones. He didn't want his own boy to have to suffer like that.

He remembers leaving Ireland at the age of twenty-two with seven pounds in his pocket. He has survived through the Church. He thinks of himself as a crusader, a soldier in the Army of God. All his life, he has felt an energy, a sort of fever, sealed too tightly, one that has sometimes escaped his control. At times, he has almost lost his temper even with his own God. He thinks of the famous lines: 'Else a great prince in a prison lies.' His favourite ones are Blake's:

> *Bring me my bow of burning gold:*
> *Bring me my arrow of desire:*

> *Bring me my spear:*
> *O clouds unfold!*
> *Bring me my chariot of fire.*

He has refined his own name, dubbed himself anew in a moment of pride and brilliance, drawn himself close to Lord Nelson by using his title, Duke of Brontë. He has reinvented himself.

He recalls the blacksmith pointing him out to a passerby who had brought his horse for shoeing.

'See this peasant boy, with his blackened hands and face,' he had said. 'He is one of nature's true gentlemen.' He must have been six or perhaps seven and working hard for a blacksmith in his forge, bending over his fire, the sparks in the air. It was a moment he would never forget. Pride and shame: *I will become a real gentleman, I will.* It had made him both proud and aware of his miserable condition. From that moment on, he had aped his betters, watching the way they ate and dressed and, above all, what they read.

He is ashamed of his parents and of his shame – particularly of his mother, that someone would find out that she had renounced her Catholicism on her marriage to his father. In the dead of the night, with everyone sleeping, he would hear her muttering her popish prayers in Latin.

He has taught his son Greek and Latin. He has let him read freely from all the books in his library and those of the wealthier families around them. Education has been his salvation, and he hopes it will save even these poor, plain girls. He has even allowed his girls to join the boy, to take a hand at a translation of Horace or Catullus. He has found Charlotte with Byron's *Don Juan*, and remembering his own youth, he has not voiced his opprobrium.

He remembers the things his children brought back to him from their rambles on the moors: little Emily rushing into his study, smelling of wind and wildness, with a lapwing's plume, a tuft of moss. Her gift reminds him of a line from one of his poems: *Sweet Philomel and cooing dove. The milk-white thorn, the leafy spray.* Not a bad line.

He remembers the Reverend Tighe's amazement at his memory. He stood awkwardly, aware of his heavy boots, his ill-fitting trousers, his frayed shirt cuffs in the elegant parlour, before a company of amazed Evangelicals. Staring at the yellow silk curtains, the painted cream wainscoting, the silver, the flowers, he quoted passages from the Bible by chapter and verse. 'As many as are led by the Spirit of God, they are the sons of God. For ye have not received the spirit of bondage again to fear . . . For I reckon that the sufferings of this present time are not worthy to be compared with the glory which shall be revealed in us.' On and on he galloped through Romans fearlessly and without a fault, only coming to a halt when Tighe said, 'Now this is the kind of mind useful to our cause,' smiling and turning to the others with a proprietary gesture, as if he had invented him.

That which has been taken for learning, for love of the Word of the Lord, for courage, he realizes now is also rage, one that wells up within him even now and has made him act foolishly. Perhaps he should have gone into the Army rather than the Church. Does he lack the empathy that his calling requires? Is that why he is being punished? Does he not know how to love even his own girl, who has been sitting so quietly at his side?

He remembers with shame now his disapproval of his poor wife's innocent gay dress, which he had never allowed her to wear, but kept firmly locked away in a drawer.

Yet there were moments when his rage was not misplaced. He sees the crowd of raucous children, taunting the poor idiot boy and then pushing him into the dark, icy, swirling water, into which he plunged to drag the boy onto the bank and lay him down gently in the grass; he remembers rising from his bed in the middle of the night, stuffing the loaded pistols into his belt and tramping across wet moors, to succour the mill owner who had need of him during the Luddite uprising when misery had generated such hate for the machines and their masters who took away the workmen's bread.

What an unexpected boon to have no demands at all made on me, to lie here idle and resting in the quiet and the dark, these kind hands on my body, to be able to return to a state of innocence. If only this could go on forever. If only this woman could immerse me completely in warm water. Water. Holy water. I am anointed. My cup runneth over. I know that my Redeemer liveth.

A christening. How many babies has he held over the font? 'I name thee in the name of the Father and the Son and the Holy Ghost.' It continues to be a moment of joy, exhilaration, and hope for him, this entrance into the community of the blessed, though the christenings are so often followed fast by the death knell in his unsanitary parish. For a moment he is filled again with rage at the authorities who allow this to continue, who have ignored his repeated letters of complaint about the tainted water that runs down from the rotting bodies in the graves.

He feels a sort of tickling on his chest, so many places all at once. 'What is it?' he cries. The image of worms in the grave comes to him. He is being consumed. 'Help me!' he cries out.

'Leeches,' the nurse explains, 'to prevent swelling. Be still. It will be brief.'

'How many?' He wants, oddly, to know.

'Just six of them, to draw the blood,' she says.

Compared to the operation, this experience is nothing, surely, the nurse says to him in her calm, reasonable voice. When she removes the leeches, she scrapes at the wounds to make them bleed further.

'Where is my daughter? Where is Charlotte?' he cries. How could she leave him at such a moment!

Charlotte comes and sits beside her father, taking his hand. 'I am beside you, dear Papa,' she murmurs.

'Don't leave me please, darling girl,' he stammers. 'My dear, my dear, how glad I am you are there,' he says, and holds her hand tightly to his drumming heart. He reaches out to hold her close. 'I hardly wish to gain my sight, that I may keep you beside me, always, always.'

Now he hears the rustle of skirts and would like to reach

out his hand to stroke them, to cling to them. He would like to cry out once again, as he would have liked to during the operation, as his poor wife once did, 'Help me for I cannot bear it!'

CHAPTER ELEVEN

Origins

*H*e asks her to read aloud from his Bible. She opens it to the collect for the day and runs her fingers over the fine page. 'Out of the mouths of babes and sucklings hast thou ordained strength,' she reads. She imagines him swallowing the holy words like wine. Indeed, he opens his lips like a child on the Words of the Lord. The candlelight flickers on her page and on his face. The room disappears into shadow. The brown leather armchair in the corner crouches down ominously like an Unholy Beast. *Regions of sorrow, doleful wastes*. At two in the morning, they are both awake and breathe in tandem.

She remembers the moment when he had suddenly entered their small room while they were playing their game with the toy soldiers. He had another game for them, he said, bringing forth something they had seen hanging on the back of his door, a mask he had kept from his days at Cambridge. He told them to put it on, allowing them to disguise themselves, becoming anonymous. What careful answers the girls gave to his questions; only the boy dared speak his mind. He spoke proudly of the differences in their bodies. Now she has no need for a mask. She can see her father faintly in the flickering candlelight, but he cannot see her. He no longer frightens her. *Entirely at my mercy*, she thinks, and smiles slightly. Now she can speak and write freely. He is no longer watching over her; she watches over him. He is in her panopticon. She likes this reversal of roles.

She is absorbed by her task, driven onward here and now by her desire to succeed, to conquer. She will vanquish all those arrogant fools, all those hateful asses, who have passed her by without a glance. How they have humiliated her, again and again. Let the great poet eat his words! Let her employers get down on their fat knees and beg her pardon! Let her Master see what she can do. She will get their attention with this new book.

She hears him mumble the words of the *Agnus* over and over, to ward off the danger of eternal damnation.

She has heard all his stories, the different ones trotted out for different occasions in different accents. Depending on whether the listener needs to be instructed or impressed, he speaks of his early days as examples of application and diligence or of his success as a scholar, his publications of poetry, his novelettes, his letters to the press, his days at Cambridge. In his Northern Irish brogue, which sounds more Scottish than Irish to her, he stresses Carlyle's motto: *Not what I have, but what I do is my kingdom*. To the simple sheep farmers of his parish, he describes in detail the dreadful mush of potatoes and cornmeal he was given to eat, which gave him lingering dyspepsia. He never mentions the Irish relatives, especially not the Catholic mother, of course. Apprenticed first to a blacksmith, then a weaver, he had started his own school at fifteen, he tells his awed listeners.

Her friends from school, the local landowners, such as the Heatons, get nothing of the Irish origins, and instead receive the tales of Cambridge, St John's College, and Lord Palmerston, as though he had been a close friend, all in a high Tory accent.

She shares his Tory beliefs in hard work and discipline and reliance on a traditional elite. Wellington, her hero! Like her father, she was for limited emancipation of the Catholics, with their mumbo jumbo and superstitions.

'I was afraid if I didn't send some of you off, Aunt, too, would have left. It seemed the best thing for you. The school came highly recommended, you know. Who could have predicted what would happen there?' her father says.

She feels the porousness of the paper, and an idea comes scurrying into her mind like a mouse. She knows how to continue her tale. She sees the tall, lean clergyman, all in black, erect as a column in the drawing room. He believes children should not be given a taste for finery and luxury. He would burn their coloured boots, as her father once threatened to do. His name comes to her with the first three letters of her own: Bro-Bro-Brocklehurst.

That night once again she lies awake. When sleep does finally come to her, she dreams one of her recurrent dreams. She sees two strange, shadowy figures standing side by side in profile looking out the window at the grey church tower, the churchyard so crowded with tombstones that the rank weed can hardly push up between them.

They are dressed in silk gowns with high feathers in their profusion of ringlets. Half-covering their mouths, fans flutter in their gloved hands. They lean toward each other, looking out at the graveyard with a supercilious air. They have rarely had visitors of this quality in the parsonage, yet something familiar about them makes her tremble, afraid.

'You asked to see me?' she says in a quiet voice. When they turn from the window with a rustle of taffeta, lowering their fans, she realizes they are her two older sisters, dead long ago as children, and now irremediably changed. When she rushes to hold them in her arms, they stare at her as though they don't know her. They hold her from them as they look around the familiar room disapprovingly. 'What a small, dark room this is, after all, isn't it?'

All her life she has carried the memories – more scars than memories – of her suffering those ten months, at the boarding school, Cowan Bridge. There were the long walks with wet shoes, the frequent, long church services on Sundays, the bitter cold, the sole privy for seventy girls and teachers, the lack of wholesome food, the constant hunger, and above all the humiliation and anguish of watching helplessly as her eldest sister was slowly tortured and then killed.

The reality was worse than the picture she gives of it in her book, because her sister's sufferings, she is aware, would be unbelievable on the page.

She cannot describe the moment when her ill sister, suffering from the blister on her side, raised by the doctor to relieve her lungs, was thrown from her bed onto the dormitory floor by the teacher, who screamed, 'Get up, you lazy girl, get out of bed immediately!'

She leaves out how she watched the scene and listened in silence, too afraid of punishment to come to her sister's aid in the dormitory that freezing morning, the water for washing frozen in the basins by the beds. She remembers watching her dying sister struggling to dress herself properly, and how the ten-year-old Maria remained silent with Christlike patience and fortitude, hearing herself called 'slovenly and untidy' without retort, and was ordered to go about the ordinary business of her day.

Death was presented to the little girls as the great protector from sin, as the goal, the recompense toward which all children should hurry forward to claim with joy – all children, that is, except for Carus Wilson's own pampered ones. She will unmask the dreadful director of the institution. She will net him and pierce him. She will immortalize his wickedness and his hypocrisy with a dart of venom.

On the page, too, she will make Jane lie in the arms of her dying friend, as Charlotte would have liked to do in her sister's, whom their father finally took home to die. She would have wanted to hold her hand, to soothe her pain, as her older sister had done so often for her, for all of them, as their mother lay dying. She would have liked to kiss her on her smooth, pale cheek before she departed for ever. Why had she not been able to keep her safe?

CHAPTER TWELVE

❦

Progress

Since she was sent away to school as a young child, she has often been homesick. It comes to her now, alone with her father in the dark, that old feeling of abandonment, the longing for home, for a mother she has never really known, for her dead older sisters, for her brother as he was as a boy, for the closeness of her family as she once knew it. She remembers how she went out into the world to earn her bread for her brilliant brother, so that he could go up to London to become a painter. It was all so much harder than she could have imagined.

❦

Her tooth aches and when she bends her head lower to her page, it is worse. Yet she realizes that she wants only these calm, autumn days in this strange city, days of uninterrupted work in these small, shuttered rooms. She does not want her past, not even her closeness with her brother, nor the brief affection of her black swan.

Sometimes, in the cool of the September night, she takes a blanket from her bed. She collects her pencil and her notebook and wraps the blanket round her bare legs and feet. She sits in the moonlight by her father's bed and writes. He seems aware of her presence, whether he wakes or sleeps. He seems to talk more to the dead, her mother, her sisters who are gone, or her absent brother. He lies very still, as the doctor has requested, even though his eyes are no longer bandaged. Gone is his old impatience with her. Her name now comes frequently to his lips. 'Charlotte! Charlotte! Are you there, child?'

She has her small, square notebooks, where she writes, hardly seeing the words. Her toothache is better, and since she has been writing her bowels, so often obstructed, have moved regularly, as though they were directly connected to the flow of words from her mind onto the page.

'Charlotte, come closer,' he calls her to bend over him.

'What is it, Papa?'

He gropes, finds her arm, draws her nearer still. 'Get rid of her,' he says.

'What? What did you say?'

'Tell that woman we don't require her services any longer. We can manage alone. An unnecessary expense,' he whispers, drawing her closer to him, her arm like a bird's wing in his hand.

'Soon, soon, Papa,' she whispers close to his ear, thinking of bathing his old, decaying body, the bedpan.

'A few days will suffice,' he says firmly, his hand touching her face, her neck. 'An unnecessary extravagance we cannot afford. We can manage alone. Just leave the pan near me. I can do it myself.'

'If you wish, Papa,' she whispers hesitantly.

'I do wish,' he says.

⸎

Her girl-child grows up fast and searches for independence. She will advertise, find work elsewhere, leave the school, Lowood, where her memories are of cruelty and neglect mingled with kindness and learning. The good Miss Temple gives Jane a brooch. A response arrives in the form of a letter from a Mrs Fairfax of Thornfield Hall. A position as governess is offered. She has the chance of moving on.

⸎

'We will not require your services any longer,' she says to the nurse when she enters the room. The woman just stares at her. 'The doctor said—' she starts to say.

'We will manage on our own,' her father says from his bed with his old voice of authority. 'We will pay you until the end of the week, of course,' he adds.

'As you wish,' the nurse replies, and drops a brief curtsy. Charlotte thinks she looks rather relieved, as she turns to gather up her things. Now that the woman is leaving, she thinks she might miss this Humber.

'I hope you will find your little girls well,' she adds as the woman comes to say goodbye, and Humber smiles at her and takes her hand.

'Good luck,' she says. 'Good luck to you with your writing, Miss. It must almost be a book by now. Perhaps I will read it one day.'

'Indeed, I hope you will,' Charlotte dares to say, but in truth she cannot imagine her words in print reaching even this woman.

❧

While she was working as a teacher at Roe Head, where she had once been a pupil, she dared to send off a packet of her poems with an ardent letter expressing her desire to write to Southey, the poet she admired so much. His response arrived more than three months later. When she read it, she wrote on the envelope, 'To be kept forever. My twenty-first birthday.'

❧

The poet laureate's response had arrived at the end of a long day of toil, a day of listening to the stultifying recitations of her thick, dull pupils. How she hated them! The Misses Lister, Marriot, Walker, and Cook seemed unable to comprehend the difference between an article and a noun. She had felt obliged to exhaust herself with a long walk after tea, coming back and slipping silently upstairs to the dormitory for a moment of blessed solitude, drawing the dark curtains around her bed.

She lay there deliciously lost in an erotic fantasy of Zamorna, her young duke and demon, coming to her, plumed and sabred, bare chest heaving, hair dishevelled, fiery eye kindling her desire, when Sister Margaret, the eldest of the family of five sisters who ran the school, poked her head through the curtains, shaking her ringlets with enthusiasm and waving the letter in the air. 'A letter for you, my dear,' she crooned, smiling kindly, believing, no doubt, she was lightening her favourite teacher's load.

She rose fast from the bed and took it eagerly, her heart already knocking. Letters were what kept her alive then. Seeing the name of the sender, the walls of the dormitory, even the evening view of the soft valley outside, seemed to swing around her so that she feared she might fall and had to clutch onto the end of the iron bedstead before her.

But with the door closed behind Sister Margaret, she sat with the letter, unable to open it. She huddled in the silence of the bare, narrow dormitory. She clutched the letter to her thudding heart, too fearful to tear it open, preferring now not to know, to keep the hope of a favourable response alive.

Too soon, Sister Margaret's voice called her forth to attend to her evening duties. She had missed her opportunity. Now there remained Miss Lister's clothes to be mended, a dumb geographical problem to be solved for some dolt, some ass's nightcap to be found. She clenched her teeth against the misfortune of this wretched bondage to the daily grind and thought of her brother, who had remained so blithely free.

It was only later that night that she read the words from the famous poet in the flickering candlelight. And what terrible words! They were burned into her mind forever. There was really no need to keep the letter for herself but rather for posterity to judge. 'Literature,' he kindly informed her, 'cannot and should not be the business of a woman's life . . .'

For a long time she could not sleep. She lay there in her white flannel nightgown, the light of the moon shining on her face. She was exhausted after a long, mindless day with her pupils, her long walk, her riotous emotions, and yet thoughts continued to race through her head. She turned back and forth, praying to God for some relief. She had long ago refused to take any remedy for the sleeplessness that so often afflicted her and still does. Watching her brother sink into stultified stupidity after imbibing some opiate, she was wary of such a remedy. So she lay there, praying to God for peace of mind. At first light she rose and took up her pen. With furor, the nib scratching at her page, she wrote the poet her most dutiful response, a response steeped in irony and rage. 'In the evenings, I confess, though I try not to, I do think . . .' she wrote.

CHAPTER THIRTEEN

Governess

She left her home, her dear Emily and Anne, her brother, her father, with such misgivings, afraid she had made a terrible mistake, and then, when she came upon the place of her new employment, in the spring sweetness of the day, all the extravagant hopes of youth revived. She was twenty-three. She leaned out of the carriage window, the sun on her face, and saw the broad, clear front of the house, all the windows thrown open, two maids gazing out in black dresses and white caps. Perhaps they were looking for her?

She imagined the children might run across the lawn to welcome her with curtsies and perhaps even a bunch of wildflowers they had picked for her. Her employers might take her to their hearts. She knew them socially, after all. They had friends in common. They were industrialists who had risen in the social scale, *nouveaux riches*. They could hardly treat her as a servant. She was the educated daughter of a distinguished clergyman.

The place stood in a privileged spot, sheltered from the north and exposed to the warm south, at the end of a long driveway, shaded by great trees. It seemed to have come straight out of one of her Angrian stories. From the terrace where she stood waiting to enter, she could see across the valley of the Lother as far as the river Ayre.

Ushered through the grand drawing room, through a library, and along the three-arched passageway linking them, she did not become aware of the true situation immediately. Her employer, a tall, big-boned, handsome woman who did not need rouge to enhance her charms and who was obviously carrying yet another child high up beneath her blue taffeta dress, greeted her with a fussy affability. 'How lovely to meet you,' she said, half-turning from the big bowl of spring flowers she was adjusting with a beringed hand. 'I'm so glad you have arrived on such a fine day. Did you have a good journey? You must meet my little ones.' She seemed to have forgotten that they had already met and went on volubly without waiting for a response, calling for her two youngest children to meet their governess. She held the solid boy squirming on her knee and wiping his sticky mouth and hands on her gown. The little girl sat on the pink, silk-covered loveseat at her side. The mother spoke of their recent ailments, their delicacy, their susceptibility to colds, their cleverness, their aptitude, especially that of the boy, whom she called a 'flower of the flock', one who even at his young age knew the difference between right and wrong. She admitted that he might at times be a little high-spirited, but then, what boy was not? As for the girl, well, she was perhaps a little nervous, a little sensitive, and a little highly strung. Of course, both of them were used to the most tender of treatment and were unaccustomed to hearing a harsh word.

Was this good news? she wondered. She told herself that it would take time to get to know this place. She would try hard to please: she would be diligent; she would win them over, and surely they would see what mental wealth, what moral certainty, she had to offer. She thought of all the books she had read, her French, her talent for painting. She thought these people would gradually see inside her; they would be interested, surely, in the value of her mind.

She caught a brief glimpse of the master of the house, a blond, ruddy, and energetic-looking man who was coming down the stairs with rapid steps, a riding crop in his hands, a large Newfoundland bounding at his side. He impressed her rather more than the wife. Sticking his crop in his boot and restraining his dog with one hand, he was gracious enough to extend the other to her and welcome her with sincerity and good humour.

It was only when she realized that the maid was leading her up to the third floor, the servants' quarters, that the crash came, a rapid descent from a high cliff of expectations. Alone in the room, she looked down through the paned Georgian windows and watched the guests' carriages arrive. She listened to the sound of the men's and women's gay voices as they descended and entered the house. She heard a woman say, 'You will not!' followed by a man's laughter. No servants, these. What had she done to deserve this lonely fate? Why was she destined for nothing but toil and solitude?

The next morning she rose, hungry and filled anew with expectations. She would show them all what she knew. Had she not read all of Scott, Bunyan, Byron, Milton, the Elizabethans, and even George Sand? Her employers probably had no idea who George Sand was!

By the end of breakfast, which she took with her two very young charges on the second floor, in the nursery, it came to her that she was to be the *nursery* governess. She was in charge only of the two youngest children and not the older two. There would be no need for Byron or Scott. She would be obliged to eat upstairs in the nursery-cum-schoolroom on the second floor, with her turbulent charges, or in her own room and not, as she had hoped, with the family or their many guests whom they entertained below in the dining room.

She sat stiffly at the table, starving but unable to swallow a mouthful of oatmeal all through this first meal, or to enjoy the radiant scene of the park in the May sunshine beyond the three bay windows. It was only thanks to the good-natured Irish housemaid that her charges were kept at the table rather than under it, and the food from flying through the air.

One hand on her waist, the other holding firmly on to the platter of fried eggs and rashers, the housemaid turned her head and said to the little boy, 'Now you stop playing with your porridge or you won't get any of these nice fresh eggs.' This command, which had consequences, he listened to. Humiliated, hungry, her hands shaking, their governess was obliged to wipe the boy's smutty nose and shovel his thick porridge into his mouth. She rose again and again to fetch the little girl's pinafore from the floor.

'If you don't behave, I'll have to tell your Mama,' she said finally, and tucked a napkin around the stout little boy's thick neck. He looked up at her with his wide face, waved a plump arm in the air, and shouted, 'You are a servant and stupid, and she won't believe you. She will punish you instead!'

She understood then that these people would never know her, nor the children look up to her. On the contrary. She was simply a necessary commodity, brought in to perform certain services, which she was beginning to suspect herself quite unfit to perform. Her employers hardly glanced at or addressed a word to her or, if they did, treated her with obvious condescension. 'Would you mind fetching my shawl, my dear? Like a fool I've left it in my bedroom,' a guest asked her as she sat in her deck chair on the lawn.

On her first morning she was brought in for a brief interview with the housekeeper and given a lengthy list of chores to be performed. 'Of course, in your spare time, there will be the sewing to attend to,' said the woman, who had a frizz of false curls on her forehead, which reminded Charlotte of her aunt's. It was made abundantly clear that she was here to perform the greatest possible quantity of labour for the least amount of money.

When she wrote home to Emily and Anne, telling them not to show her letter to her father or her aunt, informing them that her days began at six and ended at eleven, she suspected that they would not believe her. It was slavery: thankless work without dignity. The two small, rude children had no notion of obedience. Unable to resort to any sort of punishment, she had only the weapons of perseverance and firmness. She was obliged to resort to holding the little boy down on the floor until his fury abated, in order to avoid his hands and feet.

She realized, too, to her consternation that, like her father, she did not enjoy the constant presence of children – or certainly not these children, spoiled, indulged in every way, who treated her with no respect, yet expected her to follow them wherever they led. The boy was principally interested in the traps he kept for birds or moles in the garden. When he rode his hobbyhorse in the house, he whipped it mercilessly and dug his heels into its flanks. To teach them anything, she was obliged to catch and hold them in their seats, while they screamed and kicked and bit and spat in her face.

They had been forbidden to play in the stable yard, because of the danger of the horses' hooves. But one morning, the little boy slipped from her grasp and ran after his older brother into it. 'Come back here immediately!' she found herself screaming. The little boy stopped, looked back at her, and grinned. He picked up a stone from the dust, and before she realized what he intended, reached back with his arm and threw it at her with all his strength. It struck her on the forehead and narrowly missed her eye.

Stepping into the schoolroom the next morning to see her children, her employer stood briefly by the fire and remarked on her governess's swollen eye. 'You have injured yourself?' the woman asked without much interest.

When Charlotte shrugged and said nothing, the boy was moved to say that he loved his governess. She praised her son's affectionate nature and sailed out of the room.

After the children had gone to bed, there was the pile of sewing to be done. She sat alone in the schoolroom, listening to the sounds of merriment, the strains of music and adult conversation coming from below. While she toiled, the others dined and conversed or danced. She could not even hide in her room with a book or take up her pen. She was expected to sit up mending or hemming or sewing dolls' clothes by candlelight, straining her already weak eyes on a tiny muslin bonnet, wee socks, or a minuscule petticoat before finally climbing the stairs to the servants' floor, where she lay awake.

During the day she slipped silently through the grand rooms. She never looked at herself in the mirrors. Occasionally, she caught a glimpse of her shadow in the grass. She knew she was growing thin. She was constantly hungry, but unable to eat at the table with the wild children. She wanted nothing fancy, not the trifles or blancmange or hare's tongue she saw being taken into the dining room below, just a moment of quiet on her own with a simple dish and a book. Above all what she missed was a new idea or a stirring thought coming from without. She became increasingly aware of intellectual stagnation. She was afraid that she might become like these people, her intellect deteriorating, her heart petrifying, and her very soul contracting.

Nor did her employer's husband show much interest. She rarely saw him except on Sundays, when the family went to church. During the week he was busy with various employments, roistering around the countryside, foxhunting or horse-jockeying. He was a practical farmer and a hearty *bon vivant*. If he caught sight of her, he would offer a cheery greeting of some kind, which would give her a momentary lift in spirits.

How different these fashionable people acted from those in her Angrian fantasies. There she could perform heroic acts herself or wait lovingly for the hero's return. Here, as the days went by, she began to wonder who she was. In the evenings, surrounded by groups of guests, she would feel most alone. She sat still in her corner with her knitting until she could not bear it, then slinked off to her own room. Her breath grew short; her hands trembled; she often found herself on the verge of tears.

Her employer admonished her one wet June morning as she followed her charges down the stairs. 'You really must endeavour to acquire a more sociable and cheerful disposition, for the children's sake. Something franker, more natural, as it were,' she said as the children ran to embrace their mother. 'Such a long face is not good for them, is it, my darlings?'

She stood there before her employer, battling with tears. The woman drew herself up and launched into one of her sermons.

'You are a victim of wounded vanity, my dear,' she said. 'You are proud and therefore ungrateful. You are, after all, paid a handsome salary, and if you don't make an effort to quell your ungodly discontent, you are likely to go to pieces on the rocks of morbid self-esteem and end up in an insane asylum.'

Humiliated thus before the children, who stared up at her with some satisfaction, she lost all self-control and burst into tears. She rushed back up the stairs and threw herself on the bed, in a passion of grief and rage. She sat weeping and drumming her fists against her knees in the window seat, studying the garden in the mist and cloud, a dismal scene of wet lawn and storm-beaten shrub. How could the woman speak to her thus!

In what way was this woman, with her animal spirits and limited mind and education, better than she? Her husband had inherited his position from his father, whose wealth and, indeed, this estate were procured by the efforts of children working thirteen hours a day. Yet she, the governess, was ordered to walk at a distance behind the family when they went to church on Sundays. Or if permitted to ride in the carriage with them, she was placed in a position far from the window and with her back to the horses, stifled to the point of sickness.

She considered leaving the place. There were moments when she would have preferred to be dead. But she decided to stay and survive. She would toil on. With the thought of her father's example, her family's affection, her intellectual and moral superiority, she determined that she would not give in; she would preserve her dignity.

Then, one July morning, there was a visit with the family to the house with the battlements. The girl, in her pink satin frock and lace gloves, was quiet for once, and the noisy boy was left behind with the maid. On her best behaviour on this summer ride in the open carriage, the girl even tried out a few words of French that she had learned from her governess. She turned her pale, small-featured face up to the sun, which shone serenely on the still, green fields. '*Quelle belle journée, n'est-ce pas, Mademoiselle?*' she said almost pleasantly. As they entered the gate, the church bell was tolling the hour.

Charlotte looked up at the grey front of the three-storyed mansion with its battlements and rookery, listening to the cawing of the dark birds that circled the sky, swooping down low into the thornbushes or taking wing, disappearing in the direction of the lonely blue hills.

Inside she stood in the entrance hall by the door, which was half glass. She looked at the suits of armour and a bronze lamp hanging from the ceiling. The amiable and garrulous housekeeper took them first through the library, then a grand dining room with one large stained glass window, a Persian carpet, and dark-panelled walls, and next through a pretty drawing room with a boudoir with white mouldings and floral carpets and red glass sparkling on the mantelpiece. She thought of snow and fire. 'Bohemian glass,' the housekeeper sang out before leading them up the oak staircase through the chambers and finally to the third floor, with its long dark corridor and muffled, low-ceilinged rooms, filled with fine old furniture.

The little girl was moved to ask if there were any ghost stories about this house. 'It looks like the perfect place for a ghost,' she said, holding Charlotte's hand tightly. The house-keeper replied that there were no ghosts but there was, indeed, a strange story the villagers told of a madwoman, the wife of the master of the house, confined up here during the eighteenth century.

⁓

It was not long after this visit that on an evening walk, her heart beating lightly if not feebly – she was still not in her twenty-fifth year, after all – the idea came to her. Desperate for a moment of solitude, she had put her turbulent charges to bed and abandoned her endless sewing, left the housemaid, and gone out without even the light of the moon to guide her, letting the starlight and memory trace her solitary path. She followed it through the wood until she came to a stone wall, where she stopped. A new power seemed to come to her from the glimmering grounds, the grey cloud blown fast across the star-studded sky. She heard the autumn wind gather its stormy swell. She drew energy from the dark, from the low wind that blew her restless skirts around her ankles, and she seemed to hear a voice saying: 'Leave this place and go hence.' She was filled with such a wish for wings, a desire to know, to see, to learn, driven by a consciousness of faculties unexercised, of longings unfulfilled.

She determined to take Emily with her, to leave Anne at home with their father and to go abroad.

All through the night she wrote and rewrote a letter to Aunt in her head. At first light, she put pen to paper. She asked, businesslike, for one hundred or even fifty pounds. She decided against France or Germany and chose Belgium, because the living would be cheaper, and she could improve her French and Italian and perhaps even gain a smattering of

German. These, she argued, would make it easier for her and her sister to attract pupils. She dared even to compare her path to her father's, when he left for Cambridge.

Still, her ambitions had been severely pruned, many of her countless illusions of early youth lost, the world of her juvenile fantasies cleared away. She had written no new poems for years. She now looked back on the years of her early youth and on the repeated discouragements she had received with a sort of stifled rage and impatience.

Six months later she would be travelling slowly through the flat Belgian fields, and she would feel exhausted after the sleepless night on the boat to Ostend, her stomach still queasy and her fingertips and toes cold in the early February morning. Emily had consented to this undertaking because of her urging, because a school would be a way for them all to stay together, and for that they needed languages. Her younger sister, she could see, was determined this time to do all she could for her family.

The countryside did not appeal to Charlotte: the lack of the open space she was accustomed to; the bare, flat, treeless fields; the slimy, narrow canals, lying coiled like sinister green snakes; the sky, low and grey. Yet she clutched her sister's hand from time to time in her excitement, filled with a quiet ecstasy of freedom and enjoyment. She flattered herself that she was now going to see something of the world. She had a feeling of desolation mingled with a strong sense of the novelty of their situation. She felt whirled away by magic and dropped into an alien place.

She thought of the school she would be attending, of what she would learn, of the exquisite pictures and venerable cathedrals she would see there. Speaking another language, learning again, not teaching, she would be able to pass through these months with quiet diligence with her sister at her side. Why were such ordinary things so difficult? Why was it such an agony to be confronted by new people, new sights, new situations? She would turn to the Lord and ask for help. *God help me. Let my suffering not get the better of me.*

Despite her determination, nothing prepared her for what she was to encounter on the rue d'Isabelle.

CHAPTER FOURTEEN

❧

Thornfield

Jane walks into town to post a letter for the housekeeper, Mrs Fairfax. In the gloaming she thinks she hears the Gytrash on the road, but the long-haired black-and-white dog passes her by and the horse is ridden by a man, not a ghost. Man and horse slip and fall to the ground. When the man rises, Jane notices the considerable breadth of his chest. He puts his heavy hand on her shoulder and limps as she guides him to his horse. She hands him his whip, and he proceeds. She goes on to slip the letter in the box.

❧

Thus she describes Jane's first meeting with her Master at Thornfield, Mr Rochester. She has her walk with him in the garden, as she has done with Monsieur H. She lets her speak up, as Charlotte has not dared to do. She lets Jane say to her employer, who is much older than she, 'I don't think, sir, you have a right to command me merely because you are older than I, or because you have seen more of the world than I have; your claim to superiority depends on the use you have made of your time and experience.'

On the page she dares, like the inventors of Pamela and Rebecca before her, to invent lively exchanges for Jane and Mr Rochester. Jane takes the moral high road, as Pamela and Rebecca have done before her.

※

It comes to Charlotte now: the mysterious sounds in the dark, footsteps, cries from the attic, the incomprehensible servant, an inexplicable fire in the night, a mirthless laugh, Grace Poole stolidly sewing on the rings of a curtain, and behind Grace Poole, the mad wife, locked away in the attic. And all of this within the three unities of place, time, and action, just as her professor had instructed.

She lets her Jane be happy with her Master, gratified to have this new interest in her life, her destiny expanding at Thornfield, the great house where she has come to be a governess.

It comes to her, as she sits in the half dark beside her suffering father and writes about Jane's longing for Mr Rochester, her Master, a married man. Jane, too, is summoned to her dying aunt by letter.

Jane has watched the fancy guests, among them Blanche Ingram, arrive at Thornfield. Blanche rides beside Mr Rochester in her purple riding habit, her veil streaming and gleaming in the breeze with her raven ringlets, her trinkets, and all her accomplishments. She feels how the other woman fans the flame of Jane's passion and how she is consumed with desire.

She writes these scenes of jealousy and loss, describing the guests, the game of charades, Blanche Ingram as the bride, the terrible jealousy Jane feels. But she makes Mr Rochester leave his guests and find Jane, as she tries to slip through the shadows of the room, noting her sadness and watching as a tear trickles down her face.

Jane, too, as Charlotte did for Madame H., feels nothing but contempt for her rival, the venal Blanche Ingram, who loses interest in Mr Rochester when, disguised as a gypsy woman, he tells her his fortune is not what she thought.

Jane leaves Thornfield, believing Mr Rochester will wed her rival. She goes back to Gateshead, the place of her childhood, to find Mrs Reed dying but unchanged in her sentiments toward her. Mrs Reed, though able to see, has difficulty recognizing Jane. It is Jane who can gaze on her now, not she on Jane. After her aunt's death, Jane returns to Thornfield and, filled with an unknown joy, she meets her Master at twilight on the stile in the glimmering light. He is sitting there with a book and pencil in his hand. She confesses her feelings for him for the first time. She tells him that where he lies is her home, her only home.

Jane is tempted once again by the bigamous Mr Rochester's promises of a life of ease and love, by his pleas to save him from a life of vice and lust. 'Who in the world cares for you? Or who will be injured by what you do?' he asks her.

'I care for myself!' she cries.

VOLUME TWO

Haworth
1846–8

CHAPTER FIFTEEN

Stalled

She lifts her pencil and looks up from her notebook, listening to the great-grandfather clock chime the hour on the stairs as the rain beats down on the house and the weather draws its breath. It has seemed to rain every day since their return home. A west wind roars round the house. She listens to its notes and feels its pressure against the house, something twisting and searching, like the crying of restless spirits. She hears her sisters' pencils scratching, the click of the servants' needles, something clattering on the roof. Their brother has slipped out of the house and disappeared into the fog, leaving them all to wait anxiously for his return. She attempts to continue with her tale, but she cannot see her way forward anymore. Since returning home to Haworth with her father, confined to the house, she has not written a word. After writing for weeks in Manchester with hardly a pause, she is now without an idea, an image, a thought. Now that Jane has left her Master at Thornfield, leaving behind her trunks packed for her honeymoon voyage, her string of pearls, Charlotte cannot advance, either.

She reads over the last pages again and again: the terrible tearing of the veil in the night; the two strangers straying ominously among the hillocks and headstones near the church; Mason with his sallow skin, shivering despite his heavy coat in the cold English air; the drama of the declaration in the small, empty church; the answer to the question that is never answered about there being an impediment to this marriage: a wife. But how is she to bring all of this to a satisfactory conclusion for her readers, if not in her life? Where will Jane go on her own without letters of recommendation, money, or even shelter? What will become of Mr Rochester? What will become of his mad, violent wife?

She looks across this familiar, orderly room with its clean, scoured sandstone floor, the plain, well-polished, walnut dresser, the old-fashioned chairs, the cupboard with glass doors, containing the books, the pewter plates against the wall. She stares at the familiar painting on the wall, John Martin's towers, the ruins of a grand palace in moonlight.

Their old servant sits up with them at the mahogany table, knitting a grey sock with four needles. Now and then she sings a familiar stanza: 'Why did they send me so far and so lonely, Up where the moors spread and the grey rocks are piled?'

Charlotte's two younger sisters assume identical postures, bent over their own books. From time to time Emily looks up at her and Anne, her expression all life and earnestness.

Her large blue-grey eyes show a certain strength of character, a flash of independence, which Anne does not, perhaps, possess. They are full of humour, quickened into flame by a flash of indignation in her clear, pale face, as they mirror what she is writing. *Such a clear, honest, English face.* Anne's violet eyes and fine eyebrows and almost transparent complexion make her the pretty one among them, appealing and vulnerable in a way that invites sympathy.

Her sisters, too, are writing their second novels, though the first ones have still not been accepted. All three volumes have been sent out and rejected again. They continue to send out the same brown paper parcel, after crossing out the name of the previous publisher. Their poems have not sold, though they have been favourably reviewed. Yet all three of them have gone on writing and discussing their work among themselves, despite the lack of success. They have even paid to advertise the poems, using the words of one of the favourable reviews.

What determination, sturdiness, and self-reliance – or is it folly? Charlotte wonders, as she looks at her sisters at work, the youngest with her desk on her knees. She is as convinced of the merit of their work as of their diligence. Pale, grave, thoughtful, almost severe in their dark dresses, Emily and Anne look distinguished and intelligent. She can see that they have passed through something that has formed and linked them indissolubly. It is in the gravity of the way they sit and talk and in their laughter. It is in them even when they are not looking at each other.

Their father's eyesight has continued to improve, and he has been able to take back some of his duties from his kind

Irish curate, Arthur Bell Nicholls, who has relieved him during his blindness. Still, the problem of money remains, as their brother spends anything he can come by on drink or opiates, and none of the girls has any employment. They no longer speak of the school they had once dreamed of establishing in the parsonage. With the brother at home, a shiftless, dissipated wreck, an albatross around their necks, such a project is unthinkable. They dare not even invite their friends to visit.

Charlotte sips from her cup of tea, now cold. She sighs and says, 'My life is passing me by. Here I am thirty, and yet I have achieved nothing, nothing! Am I being punished for going back to Brussels so recklessly after Aunt's death?'

'Nonsense,' Emily says in her abrupt and practical way. Their gazes meet, and Charlotte feels suddenly younger, more hopeful, looking into her sister's beautiful, tired eyes. 'We have our work – no one can take that away from us. No matter how exhausted or sad I feel, we have our writing, and that changes everything. And we have one another, after all.'

The servant nods and smiles approvingly at these three young women she thinks of as her own bairns. 'Indeed, you do,' she says. Since her arrival in the family, these girls have been close. They have kept one another alive with their affection for one another and for their brother. She can still see them as young things, holding hands and running out together along the broad, sunny walk. They would scamper across the moors, the brother, small as he was, running on ahead, the red head catching the sunlight. He would shout, 'Catch me if you can!' and the girls would go after him, picking up the younger ones when they tripped, thrust out of the house in flannel dresses even in bad weather. 'Exercise is good for them,' the grim parson would say if she protested, pleading to keep them indoors on bitterly cold days.

She remembers them sitting huddled close by the fireside in the evening and listening to some old tale she would tell of the fairies and wee folk, tiny phantoms who frequented the leaves of foxgloves in the hollow, emerging out of ferny dells in the moors and frolicking in the beck on moonlit nights. How they would beg her for one story after another – the more violent, the more mysterious and magical, the better. She told them of the days before the mills had come in, when all the wool spinning was done by hand in the houses. She repeated all the folklore her grandmother had told her: stories of the Gytrash, the malevolent spirit who takes the form of a large dog or horse and leads people astray. She has gossiped freely about the notables of the area: the Heatons ousted from Ponden Hall for a while, the rightful heir left shamefully uneducated, a rough boy; the heiress, Elizabeth Heaton, dying young and her baby girl perishing rapidly after her; Elizabeth's misalliance with her delivery boy, tales of grand places that are no more.

Now she listens to them as best she can, though her hearing is diminishing, as the three girls read their work to one another, once their father has retired to bed. They walk up and down, arm in arm, making up plots, wild stories, laughing, encouraging one another, commenting, criticizing.

Sometimes she recognizes details: a place or an object. Indeed, they have even used her in various ways, though she herself has not much book learning. There are housekeepers in several of the books, sensible women who know much of the family's stories – and what wild stories they are! One housekeeper tells the family's story to a tenant who comes to stay in the house. She sits with her sewing or knitting – as she is doing now – and tells most of the tale. Another, in Charlotte's new book, receives the governess who mistakes her for the lady of the house and treats her with kindness and courtesy, even though she opposes the girl's marriage to the master of the house.

Of course, the three girls often disagree and sometimes dispute, but they are never unkind or petty in their comments.

They have often stepped in to take her place, indeed to nurse her, when she has been ill or injured, slipping on the ice in the dark and breaking her leg one evening and left alone in the street until her groans alerted a passerby.

Miss Emily has taken over the bread making, kneading the dough with her German grammar open at her side – perhaps the reason for the hard, crusty bread. She does the ironing, too, in the upstairs room, banging the iron down on the shirts with energy. They have brought in a young, gormless girl to help her. They have often insisted on taking over all her work, keeping her on in the house despite the efforts of the aunt, who once banished her to live with her sister for several years.

The housekeeper rises slowly now, thankful to be among her beloved girls. Her left leg still hurts and the knee swells when she stands on it for any length of time, though she does not like to speak of it. Ah! How her old body fails her. It makes her furious not to be able to do the things she once could. She frets and fumes. 'Now where have I put my glasses? I had them a second ago,' she asks her girls, shaking her head at her stupidity.

'On your head,' Miss Emily says, laughing at her. She claps her hand to her head and finds them perched there! She spends her time hunting for lost objects, while these girls spend theirs hunting for the right words. Yet in her heart she still feels young. When she sees her face in a mirror, it shocks her. *Who is this old, wrinkled woman?*

She feels no one knows quite as well as she does how to do the housework. Besides, she would so like to help and protect these poor girls. *God give me the strength to continue, the courage to go on.*

She lays her knitting in its basket, wraps her shawl around her shoulders, tells them all, as she would when they were young, to go to bed. They stare up at her with reddened, haggard eyes and shake their heads. Their household hours have always been early ones, thanks be to God, and the parson is already in his bed sleeping soundly and not worrying his poor old head over his boy.

She knows, though, that Miss Emily, particularly, likes the quiet hours of the night. She hears her moving about sometimes, muttering to herself, or even striding out into the moonlight with her big, stupid dog. She hears her whistling out there to him, striding around the garden, hands behind her back, like a boy. She seems afraid of nothing in the natural world and has separated fighting dogs, branded

107

herself with a red hot poker when bitten by a rabid one, and even punched her own in the face for disobedience. She is the only one strong enough to drag her brother up the stairs when he returns besotted from the Black Bull, laying him down on his bed and pulling off his boots, covering him over tenderly. What would they do without her?

She wonders how Miss Emily has endured watching her brother slowly disintegrate, with only brief moments of reprieve. How has she continued helping so cheerfully and competently with the household tasks, her large dog, her self-absorbed father, her besotted brother, and managed to go on scribbling into the wee hours of the night? She seems to delight in her own company. This summer, when her morning chores were done, she spent whole afternoons lying motionless on the green grass at the foot of some old tree with nothing before her but the blue of the sky, a cloud drifting by.

Since the parson's return from Manchester, things have become even worse. The boy spends all day in bed. He has managed to set his bedclothes on fire, and without Miss Emily's intervention they would all have been burned in their beds. It was Miss Anne who happened to pass by his door and spot the flames, but she had not succeeded in rousing her brother. It was Miss Emily who had had the presence of mind to rush down to the kitchen for a ewer of water, drenching the bedding, pulling down the bed hangings, and throwing her brother unceremoniously into a heap in a corner of the room. She can still see the bedclothes alight, Master Branwell lying on his back, unconscious in all the hullabaloo. How much longer will these girls wait up for him tonight?

CHAPTER SIXTEEN

Childhood

Sitting up with her sisters at her side, waiting for their brother, Charlotte remembers it all so clearly: the six small frightened children, five pale girls and one flame-headed boy, shut up alone in the small, dark room. They huddled together for warmth in the chilly house, haunted by unnamed fears. Outside the sole window was the waiting graveyard, the rain and wind beating against the pane, and beyond the cold village with its angular shadows and steep, slippery cobblestoned streets. She remembers their desolation, their expectation of catastrophe, their helpless longing for their dying mother, their concern for their grieving father, shut up alone in his room.

Unnaturally quiet children, they waited in the next room for their mother to die, for their father to emerge from his study, for the servant girls to call them for their supper, for the rain to stop. The eldest, seven-year-old Maria, sat in their

109

midst, her tangled, light hair on her shoulders. In her stained grey pinafore and dark dress she swung her damp, black boots back and forth, the laces trailing. She held the baby's bare, cold feet in her hand to warm them as she rocked her on her lap like a doll. The baby was Anne, who rested her head against Maria's pinafore, her thumb in her mouth, drool on her chin, her cheeks flushed and feverish. All the children had colds and they alternated coughing. The boy, too, cuddled up at Maria's side. Charlotte, five years old, sat sniffing, close beside him, only a year older than he. He squirmed beside her, his nose running, poking her in the ribs, tickling her. He could not keep still. She wiped his nose and her own with her grey handkerchief, hushed him, put her arm around him, and settled him close.

The four of them clustered together on the bed against the wall, while the other two girls, Elizabeth and Emily Jane, sat side by side on the mat, jam around their mouths, holding their scratched knees, looking up at the eldest adoringly, listening as she told them the story, one of their favourites, of Joseph, the youngest boy, with his coat of many colours, cast by his jealous brothers into a pit and sold into slavery. In her gentle, expressive voice, she told of hope, reversal, and redemption.

Charlotte can still see the bright stripes, the deep pit covered with sticks, the caravan disappearing into the desert distance. Joseph interprets the pharaoh's dreams, becomes his guide, and saves all Egypt from famine.

Aunt had stepped into the room one evening, looking large, an uncompromising stranger in a gigantic, old-fashioned cap, silk black dress, and false curls on her forehead. It was quite clear she was as loath to be with them as they were with her. She dreaded drafts, complained of the cold, stone floors, the curtainless windows, the barren, soggy moors – 'Not a tree, a flower, in this desolate place!' she muttered, pulling her grey shawl around her shoulders.

'What about the lilac and the currant bushes in the garden? What about the cherry tree?' Charlotte dared to ask.

'You ask too many questions, child. If you have nothing pleasant to say, be silent,' Aunt told them, shutting her door on them.

This sudden avalanche of six motherless children and a grim parson father stunned with grief might have been too much for anyone. Aunt grudgingly did her duty but complained constantly of the noise: the lazy, wasteful servant girls, the everlasting rain, the dark skies, the dreadful odours, and the bitter wind. 'Does the sun never shine in this place?' Aunt moaned despairingly.

When Charlotte dared to ask for her mother, Aunt responded, 'Indeed, I wish she were here and not I.' Aunt said little to the children and demanded quiet. She took her meals alone, as did their suffering father. She favoured the boy, who could do no wrong, and the youngest, Anne.

Though Charlotte was his elder by more than a year, Branwell, the boy, was the little king, always the centre of the family's attention, even her mother's. Charlotte sees her now, a beautiful shadow standing against the window at twilight in the parlour of the parsonage, her head thrown back, smiling up at him, lifting him high with delight. The lingering sunlight plays on his small, delicate head and his laughing eyes, which resemble his mother's, though he has his father's flaming Irish colouring.

Aunt would make sure he got the best morsels of meat, whenever they were allowed any, or the choicest piece of cake. 'Don't eat so much of that,' she would say to the girls, snatching away a plate of something particularly tasty to keep for the boy. Or again, 'Come now, let us tidy up the room and keep up a good fire; you know your brother likes one.'

Charlotte would watch as he sidled up to stroke Aunt's plump arms. She would smile down at him, tousle his hair, lift him into her lap to nestle contentedly against her large bosom. He knew how to bring her the first spring snowdrop, to hold it up to her face. 'For you,' he would say delightfully, as she sat huddled over the fire for warmth. 'I like your curls, Aunt,' he would say, staring up with apparent sincerity at the frizz of her false front of what she called auburn hair. When he impudently asked for a pinch of snuff from the gold snuffbox, one of the few treasures she had brought from Cornwall and kept proudly on her mantelpiece, she let him take one. When he sneezed loudly and dramatically and made a play of rolling around on the floor, she smiled at him indulgently.

Aunt put the girls to work with the cooking, the making of beds, the dusting, and the sewing, explaining grimly they would need to know how to make themselves useful if they were to survive. Without the mother's extra fifty pounds a year, money was tight. She told them that plain girls without a dot were not likely to marry. Destined at best to be teachers or governesses, they must prepare for their fate.

Charlotte conjures them all up sitting in Aunt's airless room, the windows firmly closed on any possible draft, only the baby girl allowed to play on the floor with her toys. While the others hemmed and turned and made their samplers as best they could, all through the long afternoon, Aunt sat tight-lipped and severe, probably dreaming of her sunny home. She read aloud to them from her mad Methodist magazines, terrifying them with their view of hellfire and damnation.

CHAPTER SEVENTEEN

❧

Waiting

*E*mily thinks how the pains of love have ravaged the three people dearest to her. Anne has been the most valiant, keeping her loss to herself and going on with her work. Charlotte, she fears, still longs for her professor. Emily glances at her sister's censorious face and wonders if she is still sorrowfully waiting for letters from him. Is she still writing to her Master? Has he responded? She has read some of Charlotte's poetry recently. She thinks of the lines: *Even now the fire / Though somewhat smothered, slacked, repelled, is burning, At my life's source.*

Branwell, in his position as a young tutor, was seduced by his employer and then discarded for false reasons, just as Emily has made Catherine Earnshaw do when spurning her Heathcliff.

Emily stares at Anne's hair, dampened and smoothed down, which gleams with a clear light when she moves her round head. When she raises her eyes to the lamp, her translucent eyes become milky blue. She stares at the small moths that have emerged out of the darkness and become prisoners inside the lethal glass around the lamp.

Emily leans her thin cheek up against Anne's, and Anne closes her eyes. *Poor, dear Anne. So brave. Still waiting for him.* Emily says the others should go to bed. She is accustomed to bringing her brother home.

From the start she has known better than her sisters how to handle him. 'What do we do with your brother?' her father had asked. Emily gave her response anonymously from behind the mask, as they all had been asked to, when she was six: 'Reason with him, and if he won't listen, whip him.' But no one had ever reasoned with him, and perhaps it would not have made any difference if they had.

Both her sisters refuse her offer to wait up alone. They could not sleep in any case. 'We will wait for him together,' Charlotte says firmly but with a dispirited sigh. She has little pity left for him. She turns her back on him when he enters the room, as though she cannot bear the sight of him. Why has she turned against him so completely? Why is she so preoccupied with her own small problems of love when her brother's are so much more serious? Still, Emily pities her.

It was out of pity for Charlotte, a fear that she might make herself ill after suffering for two years from unrequited love, that she had agreed to publish her poems prematurely. Still, Emily cannot forgive her for exposing her most secret experiences to the public. It was not that she had never intended publishing them, but she had no desire to expose their mystery at that moment. Indeed, though they have favoured her, commended her originality, her power of wing, have expressed what she knew in her heart – that Ellis Bell had the strongest voice – the reviewers have not understood the spiritual quality of her own vision. And why were none of her brother's poems included? Several of his poems were perhaps even superior to Charlotte's, yet she had never allowed any of his work to be included in the volume.

Since she has come back from Manchester, Charlotte has seemed more cheerful. She has read them some of her new book. This *Jane Eyre* is the best thing she has written. Emily waits impatiently for the next chapter. Yet this evening, waiting for their brother, Charlotte seems so dispirited, disapproving, and sad. Does she see in her brother's mad desire a dreadful mirror image of her own incoherent pleas to her Master?

Charlotte has criticized her own *Wuthering Heights* as being too extreme, too melodramatic, yet surely Charlotte, too, has gone to the extreme. Mr Rochester's mad wife, who lurks on the top floor at Thornfield, setting fire to the bed hangings, ripping the wedding veil, quick with the knife and her teeth, contains some of their brother himself, as well as Charlotte's own wild desires. As for Mr Rochester, does he not come from Byron and Charlotte's early heroes like Zamorna, but also from her Belgian professor? Certainly he looks like him, has some of his impatience and willfulness, and is trailed by the scent of his cigar. By transforming her professor into a character, a country squire, Charlotte may overcome her longing. Does writing ever cure heartache and sorrow? Will this lively book, full of incident and event, enable her to get over the sufferings of the past years? Will she finish it? Will it earn enough money for her to remain at home?

ee

Anne looks up from her book and says, of Branwell, 'I'm the one who should wait up for him. I'm the most implicated in all of this. If only I had never suggested him for the position at Thorp Green!'

'How can you reproach yourself? Who else would have taken him on? He had failed at everything. Too small for a soldier and too irreligious for a curate. Without your reference, no one would have had him. On the contrary, it was most generous of you! Those awful people even lowered your salary, and I know how much you disliked it there,' Charlotte says.

'I had really become, indeed I remain, quite fond of the girls. If they had given me any real authority to counsel them, they would have learned to live proper Christian lives. And I never imagined the mother could have behaved as she did.' Anne sighs. 'It did take that naughty boy off my hands, at least.' She doesn't speak of her own secret sorrow. God, she had hoped, would surely give her some small joy in her life, but death had blighted her hopes of love. *God help me to accept my fate, to continue with courage and dignity.*

Charlotte says, 'It seemed the best to all of us at the time, you must remember. We were all so hopeful then. I wanted foolishly to go back to Brussels, and Emily was quite happy to stay at home on her own with her animals and Papa. You took Branwell off our hands, after all. What else would he have done but stay here idle, drinking and causing trouble?'

'I did try to give him a fair picture of the family,' Anne adds, 'but I'm afraid anything I might have said had the opposite effect. Certainly he has never listened to me.'

Charlotte looks at her sisters, sitting side by side with the elderly woman who has looked after them for so many years. She realizes who must rescue Jane when she leaves Mr Rochester: sisters, of course, two sisters like her own, or two women like her two best friends, Ellen and Mary, from her school days. They have given her courage in their different ways with their example and their love. They have rescued her from despair again and again. It is women, she thinks, looking at her brave and beautiful sisters and her old and faithful servant, who have enabled her to survive. She will invent two ladies of distinction and learning, two studious sisters who study German and are obliged to go out as governesses, two sisters like those before her, two loving, intelligent women in whose conversation Jane will delight, who will shelter her in a moment of need like those two sisters who died so young, who still haunt Charlotte's dreams. She will conjure up a faithful servant with a harsh manner but a good heart and two sisters and a brother, unlike her own, one more like Ellen's, cool, clearheaded, hard, and handsome, who believes in reason, someone who is looking for a helpmate, a fellow missionary to share his load. It is they who will rescue her heroine, they and their old servant, Hannah, as she will call her, who knits away so industriously. The four of them will shelter Jane when she leaves the bigamous Mr Rochester. She sees Jane as she staggers on across the heath and falls faint with hunger at the door of their house, which she will call – what else? – 'Moor House'.

CHAPTER EIGHTEEN

❧

Retrieval

*E*mily rises now and puts on her shawl and bonnet. She refuses her sisters' offers to accompany her. 'I can always manage him better alone, and if I don't go now, I'll never get him home,' she says. 'I'll take Keeper with me.' She bends down to touch the dog's head lightly. She is not at all sure she is as safe alone as she maintains. Her brother walks the streets with a knife up his sleeve, believing that Satan is stalking him. He is capable of sudden violence.

She feels exhausted, shaky-legged. She has slept badly, dreamed strange dreams. She has risen at dawn, stumbling barefooted down the steps into the kitchen, opening the door for the dog, the sky a faint orange-pink, the autumn air already cold. Sipping her coffee, she has studied the newspapers, which are lent to them, looking for information on their railway stocks, which are doing quite well. Charlotte would like to sell them, but Emily has refused. As in all things, she relies on her own convictions. Very early in life, she learned to think for herself. She considers she has no choice but to go after her brother now. She feels they are linked in an almost supernatural way.

It hardly seemed a coincidence to her that on the same day, 26th of May, their poems had been published, thanks to thirty-one pounds from Aunt's bequest, and her brother had left the house. She can see him vividly, dressed with such care in his green suit, his red curls carefully brushed and clustered about his high forehead, his fine Roman nose and long patrician upper lip turned upward as he danced down the street. He expected to be summoned to his wealthy and adulterous beloved, who was now free, free! Mr R., who had banished him from the side of the lady he loved so extravagantly, had finally died.

Then he had instead received the command, conveyed ignominiously by her coachman or groom, not to contact her in any way. Mrs R., apparently, had more ambitious plans. A practical woman, aware of her social position, she had no intention of spending the rest of her days with the impoverished little tutor she had dallied with briefly. Since then, Emily's beloved brother has been a broken man. From time to time he receives money from a mysterious source, most probably Mrs R., who has paid him off, money that he immediately squanders on squibs of gin or sixpenny packets of opium acquired freely at the chemist's. Like her character Hindley Earnshaw, he is deliberately drinking himself into a stupor.

She has been compelled to write about it. She has written

in her poems about separation, abandonment, and union, but it is in her novel that she has exposed her brother's folly, using his apocalyptic language, his excesses of behaviour. Her book has come to her fast. It is what she wants the world to see.

Putting on her gloves, she steps out into the damp street with her dog, an umbrella over her head. She relishes the life-giving wind, the cloak of darkness, the solitude and silence. She bends down and strokes the back of the dog's head. The autumn chill and damp restore her strength and endow her with a kind of impatience. She strides onward, trying not to shiver, to give in to everything without name or shape that causes her nervous apprehension.

Since the incident of the fire, her father sleeps in the narrow bed with her brother to watch over him as he sleeps. Is he afraid he might take his own life and theirs too, like the mad wife in Charlotte's new book? Why does her father not remove the weaponry bristling on the wall of his room? She has suggested it, but he will not part from his guns. What a strange, fierce, contradictory old man he is. Yet she loves him and prefers to remain home with him and her brother, whom she loves more than her life.

She knows her brother is seriously in debt. He cadges off friends and strangers alike, even off the woman who has spurned his love. He is in danger of going to prison because of his debts to the landlord of the inn he frequents nightly. Does she not hear stories from the families around her of violent acts by usurpers who have taken over ancestral homes and fortunes, as her Heathcliff does? She has been home for four years now, a witness to every one of her brother's mad moods.

Much of her Heathcliff and Hindley comes from the man she watches now through the pub window. She stands there with her shoes sinking into the mud, her umbrella over her head, the strong smell of alcohol and urine in the air.

Her brother sits talking to a group of men gathered around him, laughing. He appears to be telling them some amusing tale. He can be a fascinating raconteur, above all, in his cups. Unlike his sisters, he is a better talker than writer. All his life he has been encouraged to talk, to entertain, to be the centre of attention. The only boy, he is expected to speak of his exploits, to tell of his triumphs.

One of his companions rocks on his chair, throws his head back, opens his mouth wide in a raucous guffaw. Another is filling her brother's glass. Surely they must see what effect it is having on her brother? She can hear the loud laughter, a snatch of song, see someone turning to the barman and calling for more wine. Her brother is standing up now unsteadily, his shoulders stooped, his hand on the back of his chair, singing for the crowd. The bartender behind the bar in his apron is drying a glass, the mirror behind him. He, too, is joining in the song. Then her brother sinks back down onto his chair, dropping his glass, which someone scrambles to recover and refill for him.

It infuriates her to see how her brother's companions encourage him. Can they not see how ill he is? She raps on the pane angrily with her knuckles, but no one heeds her. Instead, her brother flings the glass away and seizes the brandy bottle by the neck. He tilts it back and swallows greedily. She raps harder, pressing her face to the glass, calling his name. For a moment, he looks up and even stares at her with a vacant stare, his eyes bloodshot in his bloated, red face. She knows that look all too well. She recognizes the droop of the trembling lips. He has probably taken opium. He often mixes these things recklessly to the permanent detriment of his mind and health. He leans over to cough. It is this mixing of drugs that is killing him, surely, this and the weak lungs from which they all suffer. Can his companions not see his weakened condition? Does he not even recognize her? She raps again harder and shouts his name loudly. The men around him glance toward the window and back at her brother, their faces suddenly grave, embarrassed. One of them leans down and says something to him. He glances toward the window. His face darkens as he puts his hand up his sleeve. Is he armed? Will he take her for Satan?

Passion of this kind is surely better eschewed in life. Animals, with all their passionate feelings, their blind devotions, are safer to love than human beings. She leans down to pat her darling Keeper, who stands at her side.

She will not linger out here in the rain any longer. She goes around to the front of the pub, closes her umbrella, and throws open the door. She strides into the room, her hand on her dog's collar, letting the cold air enter the smoke-filled room. A hush falls over the crowd of men, and all the eyes are on her as she goes forward toward the fire, where her brother sits with his cronies in a half circle. No one moves for a moment, no sound is heard, as everyone watches her and her big dog. Then a low murmur begins. Someone says something about women and dogs not being welcome. She goes directly over to her brother and leans down to whisper in his ear. He glances up at her, his eyes small, his gaze blank. She grasps him by the arm and tries to get him to rise. 'Help me,' she says to the man beside him. Together they get him onto his feet and his cape onto his shoulders. She puts her hand around his waist and tries to move toward the door. For a moment he resists, glaring at her, then he lets his head fall on her shoulder and slumps against her body. They move toward the door together through the crowd of staring onlookers, the dog following.

She cannot help pitying him; she suffers with her mournful boy. She understands his wish to escape into another world. She finds his sufferings as hard to bear as her own: she hears him sigh with anguish, unable to console him. She sees in this wretched life all the destructive power of excessive love. She knows he is dishonest, that he will say and do anything to obtain the drugs he craves. She knows he is spineless, without willpower of any kind at this point, and yet she cannot help but love him and will minister unto him as long as she is able, though she no longer believes he will ever recover.

By the time she gets him into the hall at home, the house is silent, though the lamp in the parlour is well trimmed, its flame straight and clear, the hearth bright. Her sisters have retired to bed, leaving the room neat. She takes up the lamp from the table and helps him up the stairs to her father's room. The door is ajar and her father is stretched out on his back in the middle of the small bed, his nightcap on his head.

Together they stand side by side at the door and watch his stertorous breathing as he sleeps. She goes toward the bed and puts her hand lightly on his forehead.

'Don't wake the poor old man,' her brother says, gently slumping against the jamb of the door.

She leads him into the small room that was once their study, where the six of them had waited patiently as their mother lay dying. He collapses on the narrow bed, and she helps him remove his boots and jacket. She covers him with a blanket, and he sidles up against the wall, his back turned to her. She lies beside him, exhausted, her limbs against his.

CHAPTER NINETEEN

❧

Branwell

Writing in her room, Charlotte hears her sister and brother return. She still misses Angria, the imaginary world of her adolescence that she shared with him. She remembers the excitement of discovering a new place, as Mungo Park had just done in West Africa. The very word *Africa* was thrilling: thick vegetation, brilliant light, the burning amber eyes of a lion in thick foliage, forgotten palaces of diamonds and gold. She still remembers the map in *Blackwood's* magazine with the account of Park's voyages of discovery: the long-sought River Niger at Segu, Silla, Bamako, and Kamalia, where he fell ill and owed his life to a stranger, first taken for dead and then returned in triumph to his wife and a huge audience in London. She whispers the names aloud: the province of Ardrah, the Calabar and Etrei rivers, the Kingdom of the Ashantee. The Kingdom of the Twelve. The Angrian Wars.

She finds herself writing her brother's name instead of the bully's, John Reed's. She confuses their brutality. It was part of her, too.

A memory comes to her violently, and she feels the blood rush to her face. Her brother must have been eight or nine and she perhaps nine or ten, a small, slender girl, recently brought home from Cowan Bridge after both her elder sisters have died.

They sit closely side by side in the small room, hunched over a tiny book, writing, drawing up maps, constitutions, laws for the country of their dreams. Her brother, his tousled mop of carroty hair hanging around his pointed face, writes fast, ink staining his fingers.

'Go downstairs and leave us alone,' the brother has decreed. Charlotte has watched with some satisfaction as Emily and Anne, holding hands, dressed identically in white pinafores over black dresses, hair punished with pins, did as they were told. They have their own games, after all, and sometimes tire of the brother's gathering armies, the huge numbers engaged, the indiscriminate slaughter.

She and her brother are alone now in the small room with the sole window that looks onto the church and the graves, the table where they work. She feels he resembles her in a strange way. They are both slight of build, nearsighted, delicate, but her brother is bright and beautiful with his red hair, freckles, and brilliant blue eyes. She thinks of him as some exotic and colourful tropical bird: a bright, many-plumed parrot. He shines in the family firmament, whereas she glimmers palely, almost invisible, a moon shadow beside him. The moon to his sun, she shines only with his reflected light.

At times he favours one sister and at times another, but she, now the eldest, is often the chosen one. For this giddy moment, she is the one allowed to bask in his reflected glory, in the excitement of the tale that is far more real to her than the dull reality around her. She no longer hears the wind outside, feels the cold in the small room, or sees the pale light. Above all, the crowded graveyard with its many headstones and weeds, the church crypt with all the dead, her mother, both her older sisters so close to the house, is momentarily forgotten.

She looks up at her brother with all the adoration of a passionate nature. She is convinced of his superiority. He is allowed to go out and play freely with the other rough children in the village, allowed to shout, to whistle, to bang doors, or to sing. No one warns him, as they do the girls, of the dangers in the outer world. What makes them believe he is invulnerable to harm?

He accompanies his father to the village nearby to buy the newspapers and sees the headlines before anyone else does, discusses the news first with Papa. It is he who received the precious gift of the toy soldiers, which he bountifully shared with his sisters and which has sparked their play.

He will sometimes, if she is good to him, generously repeat what he has learned. Sometimes.

Now they are writing their secret story in a small booklet

in tiny writing no one else can read, except with a magnifying glass. She is excited to share the story with him, to braid the imaginary threads of her mind with his. Their stories come to her at unexpected moments: when she is obliged to help like an undermaid with the household tasks in the kitchen, peeling potatoes or chopping onions, or when she sits sewing through the long, dull afternoons in the airless room with Aunt. Like music they chime in her ears, sustain her, delight her, soothe her in moments of distress. She lives for these stories, for the moments when they can make them up together.

Sometimes she thinks of it as swimming, though she has never been swimming. She imagines plunging down into the cool, pale-green depths of the sea with her brother, as they sometimes hurl themselves into the wind, arms outstretched, clothes clinging to their bodies like water, running across the heath. She thinks of them as mermaids, their bodies playfully entwined, as are their minds in the shadowy, flickering light of the underworld of caves.

All day, she wonders with pleasurable excitement what will happen next: Will the heroine really die and lie cold and alone on a dreary night in the earth? In their stories they are omnipotent.

He writes as easily with his left hand as his right, writing very fast, not caring about punctuation or spelling or even logic. She does not dare intervene to correct his errors. He lets her sign her name at the end sometimes, and if he tires he allows her to write.

'Get down on your knees and be my slave,' he says with a grin. She hesitates, but there is something so raw and beautiful about the sight of him with his white arm raised imperiously in the air that she complies. When she looks up at him, a warm feeling rises from her stomach to her throat. She knows every detail of him: his untidy, flame-coloured hair falling over the glasses perched on the end of his strong nose, the bitten nails, the faint freckles, the small stature, the adorable imperfections. Each weakness makes him seem more tender, more in need of her help. She bows her head and hears the thrilling swish of a ruler beside her ear.

'Say, "My Master, I am your slave." '

'My Master,' she says, and lifts her hands as if in prayer. He smiles a thin smile and kisses her on the lips. She feels his weight against her, the solidity of his boy body. She notices the sound of the wind, the rain beating against the window, the smell of rot and decay, and the pounding of his heart against hers.

Her brother, only eight or nine but precocious and better schooled than she, at ten, now waves his hands wildly. 'They must fight,' he says.

'Wait,' she dares to say, 'we have to say more about the place, the vegetation. Otherwise it doesn't sound real.' But he sweeps on imperiously. He gives the plotline, the events, action, details of the battle. He likes the story to move forward fast. He wants violence.

'Hush,' he says. 'They have to fight, don't you see? – with swords.' And he puffs himself up a bit, throws out his chest in his loose white shirt with the ruffle at the neck, makes the gesture with the ruler of parrying with a sword. 'This is the infernal world,' he explains grandly – an expression he has read in a book. Like her, he has already read much of Byron and Scott and even Shakespeare's *Romeo and Juliet*, *The Tempest*, and *Twelfth Night*. But Byron's satanic outcast is his main hero.

'Who will fight?' she asks, doubtfully.

'Two black giants, two princes, two outcast brothers, two fallen angels. They are in a grand palace, with jewels and a golden throne. No, it's four giants, four monsters. All brothers from the same royal house, Ashantee dukes or princes. Eight feet tall with flashing dark eyes, dark skins, dark hair, moustachios, and scars. They cut the duke's neck. They cut off his hands. The blood spurts. He falls down into the pool, down, down, down!'

She shudders, makes a face, appalled. 'No, no, too awful,' she says.

'We can always make him come alive again,' he says with a grin. She protests, 'No one would believe that. What sort of a palace is it? What time of year? What's the weather? And why are they fighting now?'

'For the throne, for power, that's all,' he says. They are both snobs. They like details of grandeur, the appointing of governors, the adventures of the aristocrats: dukes and duchesses, Wellington and his sons, but she likes to dwell upon the small details that will conjure up something larger: the swing of a walk, a black neckerchief casually adjusted, lightning splitting a tree.

'That's the way it's going to happen!' he says in a sudden passion, his cheeks flushed. Which is when he grasps a lock of her brown hair and twists it round his finger, almost lifting her small, light body up into the air. He finishes this by giving a sharp rap on her fingers with the ruler. She lets him. She would let him do anything. Her mouth tastes salty and her head aches and she is aware of the danger of such passion. Though she already suspects he possesses a quality that is dangerous to him and to her, a quicksilver quality, a wild temper, an inability to accept the unwelcome reality of the world around them, she now thinks of him as a changeling brought in to replace the real baby who once lay quiet in his cradle. He is someone who does not belong to this dutiful circle of quiet, obedient girls. The outcast, the interloper, he comes from a different world.

At the same time he is what she would be if she dared: her secret double. Her admiration and adoration will now coexist with her lucidity, her knowledge of the dark side of his nature and hers.

The father, too, hears his boy come up the stairs. Dimly he sees him stand slumped at his door. Such a brilliant, beautiful boy, his heart's darling. How could this have happened to him?

After the death of his wife and of his eldest two girls, he has withdrawn from his remaining daughters. How could he not? He could not help thinking that his favourite girl, the most brilliant and saintly, had been taken from him, that he could have spared one of the others more easily. But the boy was different, strange and almost holy.

He remembers him perched on the arm of his chair, leaning

over the page from *Blackwood's*. Branwell's red hair hangs in his pointed face, glasses misted on the tip of his nose in his excitement, and the two eldest girls sitting on the dark sofa with the three little ones huddled together on the mat, their faces lifted up with joy. The boy takes the paper from him in his haste to hear the end and exultantly reads out a passage. They all lift up their hands to applaud the success of the Tories, the aristocrats, the landed power, the Great Duke, their favourite, Wellington!

Naturally, he had not expected much to come of all that scribbling for his poor girls, though they would keep scribbling, but he had had such high hopes for his darling boy. Perhaps they all had.

He wonders if it should have been the boy he sent away to school and not the girls. There were too many of them to handle: five small girls tucked away in that cramped nursery space above the door. Still, some had suggested they send the boy away. But neither he nor his sister-in-law thought he could stand it. He had not lasted long in the local grammar school. So they had kept him close, watched over him, sheltered him, adored him. Everyone adored him, particularly Charlotte. Perhaps they all spoiled him. They feared so for him: his fits, his excitability, the great swings of joy and despair, the great sensitivity, and all the gifts.

Nothing has turned out as he expected. He had considered his son someone of such strange mental and physical energy. Such a curious boy. Nothing he ever did was predictable or without contradiction.

He remembers coming into his church early one morning

to speak to the sexton and hearing someone playing the organ, sweet sounds filling the air. When he looked toward where the sounds came, he thought it was an angel with flaming hair, bent over the keys, pulling out all the stops, his little legs straining to pump the pedals. The boy was hardly twelve years old and small for his age, barely able to reach the pedals, but he was playing the organ, filling his church with heavenly music. He could play the organ, write, draw, paint. The father has taught the son and not the daughters all he knows about the classics. All that Latin and Greek. He remembers the art teacher, hired at considerable expense – at least they all took advantage of that – the studio rented, board provided, not to speak of all the letters of introduction, all unused, the precious pennies they had all scraped up for him for the journey to London, all squandered. Left to his own devices, he was incapable of rising to the occasion. The boy – he continues to think of him as a boy, though he is only a year younger than Charlotte – was crushed with despair, remorse, surely. Perhaps the best loved always suffers most.

What is to become of him? That wicked woman! That sorcerer! She had bewitched him.

CHAPTER TWENTY

❦

Openings

Charlotte sleeps uneasily through the many cold winter nights. All spring and summer she continues to send their three books out again and again, only to see them return. The poetry book does not sell, and they decide to send complimentary copies to the poets and writers they most admire, so that at least someone will read their work. She continues to work on her new book, writing the chapters that take place in Moor House, where Jane spends time with the two sisters and their brother, St John. Emily writes her poems, irons, bakes bread, feeds her animals, walks out across the moors, and goes to church. Their father's sight, though he occasionally complains of spots before his eyes, has been much improved by his operation. He resumes his pastoral work, preaches his sermons on Sundays, and visits his parishioners.

It is a rare warm day. The three sisters sit together in the dining room after breakfast, the white bowls still on the table, the summer sun glimmering for a moment on the stone floor. Their father is already out. The summer landscape has a luminescence that he has always loved and is delighted to see again. Branwell still lies in his bed sleeping, sketching, or writing pathetic complaints to his friends about his depression, asking them for money for opium.

A letter arrives. Anne hands Charlotte the familiar brown paper packet, addressed to the three Bells, and asks her to open it. She reaches across the table, across the empty bowls of oatmeal and the milk jug with its familiar illustrations of *Pilgrim's Progress*, and takes the packet gingerly with the tips of her fingers, as though it might burn them. She places it beside her empty plate and looks at her sisters. She can see that they, too, have the same cowardly urge to let the packet lie beside the bowl unopened, to hold on to the moment, to preserve hope, as she did nine years ago with the response to her work from Southey.

'What do they say?' Emily finally asks, her mouth set.

Charlotte recalls that it is almost a year since their three volumes were first sent out together. This one comes from a little-known publisher, Newby, whom they have tried as a last resort.

She slips a knife slowly under the fold. Her sisters watch closely, sitting side by side opposite her. She notes that the letter is several pages long and takes hope. She reads the first few lines to herself and looks up at her sisters' alert faces.

'Read this. It's good news,' she manages to say, feeling herself grow old. Emily snatches up the pages and they peer at them together, reading attentively, their heads close. T. C. Newby writes from his offices on Mortimer Street that he will publish two of the volumes: *Wuthering Heights* and *Agnes Grey*, but not Charlotte's *The Professor*. Nor are his terms particularly favourable. The authors are required to advance fifty pounds, which he will refund when two hundred and fifty copies have been sold. Also, he asks for changes in *Wuthering Heights*, which is to be expanded into two volumes.

Her sisters look at each other in silence, their gaze deep and searching. Charlotte sees them as though she has never seen them before: such beautiful faces. Two graceful young women, long-necked and slender – ladies, she feels, in every sense of the word, Emily with her dog's big, ugly head, like a lion's, on her knee. There is sunlight in their hair and on their pale faces. Their eyes seem bright. A fly buzzes against a windowpane. The brindled cat jumps from Anne's lap.

'What are we to do?' the youngest asks, looking from one sister to the next.

'You must not hesitate for a moment. It's not a good offer, I admit, but it's the best we have had,' Charlotte says firmly, though she is convinced they will, they must, refuse this offer. Surely they will not leave her out?

'But what will you do?' Anne asks.

'I will send mine out once again.' She can hear the tremble in her voice. She draws herself up, rises from the table, puts the sugar bowl on the sideboard, fusses with the lid. She glances over her shoulder at her sisters, who are sitting in their dark dresses looking at each other. She turns toward them. They stare up at her for a moment, speechless, lips slightly open, the letter before them. Surely, she thinks, they will not spend their legacy to publish their faulty books without her?

Besides, she knows how stubborn and retiring Emily is, how much she is against changing a word in her text. She has not listened to Charlotte's advice on her book at all. She has never cared as much as Charlotte about presenting her work to the public. She remembers the great fuss Emily made over publishing her excellent poems.

But she goes on dutifully, attempting to be sensible and, above all, fair. 'You cannot give up an opportunity of this kind. Your book could be expanded, and might even be improved, as the publishers suggest.' *Dear God, don't let them leave me out!*

Emily replies without hesitating, in her matter-of-fact manner, her voice sounding loud, suddenly reminding Charlotte of the nurse, Humber, 'You are quite right, my dear. We must consider this offer seriously. It's the only one we have had.' Charlotte is so surprised that she bumps her toe against the leg of the table. She is obliged to sit down again, her hands in her lap, the hurt so hard. She wants to cry out in protest. Whoever would have thought of Emily calling her 'my dear' in that detached and rather superior tone of voice? She adds to the hurt, 'There's always the possibility, if you send your book out again, you might find something better than this.'

There is a new assurance in Emily's voice. She is now the one in charge. She rises and pours the rest of the milk into a

139

saucer for the cat and then resumes her seat, pushing her chair back slightly and looking at them. It is clear that it is her book, with all its exaggerations and melodrama, its scenes that disturb mental peace by day and banish sleep at night, that the publisher really wants.

A new kind of silence fills the room. Her beloved sisters seem far off. Charlotte gazes at them, as from the shore of a desert island, as their ship draws away. They have abandoned her so easily. They stare at her with unbearable pity in their eyes. The alliances have shifted once again, as they did when she left for Roe Head.

How could they do this? Without her they would never have seen their poems published or received the encouraging reviews. Did the reviewers not speak of Ellis Bell's 'power of wing'? Did this not spur her on to finish her novel? Why have her sisters succeeded and not she? Are their books any better than hers? Their faces now appear altered, less fine, less distinguished, less distinct.

Why is Emily eager to rush in so readily on such unfavourable terms? Is she willing to expand her book, to let it swell to fill the place of her own? Original though it may be, as Newby says, it has its faults. She considers Emily's mind unripe and insufficiently cultured. The characters, with their relentless implacability, lack depth, complexity, and substance. Who would believe that a man who could hang his wife's beloved dog from a tree could also be capable of passionate love for his childhood sweetheart, his Cathy?

She turns toward Anne. Surely, with her strict Christian morality, her integrity, she will put her sister's good above her own. But Anne, too, nods her blonde head and agrees with Emily: 'I suppose we have little choice.'

'We do need the money, after all, if we are to pay Branwell's debts,' Emily adds, quite illogically, for they will have to pay a considerable sum for the publication, and there is no guarantee they will ever see any of the money back. Emily rises and paces in the restricted space. Already she seems to glow with energy, to have gained colour in her cheeks and light in her grey-green eyes.

'I'll be guided by your wishes in this,' Charlotte says, pursing her lips. She can hear a note of bitterness creeping into her voice. She leans back in her chair and watches Emily reach across the table, pick up a roll, and bite on it distractedly. Her own lips are dry. She feels limp, washed out. She is aware of the faint odour of rotting drains.

Emily has always taken charge of money. She has placed Aunt's legacy in railways stocks, which have done well. Though appearing so unworldly, almost savagely private at times, she is actually the most practical, the most organized, perhaps even the most intelligent, of the three of them. Certainly this Newby seems to think so. Now she will have this, too: a published novel.

'Besides, you have almost finished your new book,' Emily adds, looking directly at her. 'You can always send *Jane Eyre* out, too.'

'Not quite,' Charlotte says, aware of the churlish, petulant sound of her voice. It is true she has recently added several chapters and brought in a new romantic triangle. Jane has discovered that the brother curate, St John, named after her father's college at Cambridge, is secretly in love with a beautiful heiress, Rosamund, but will not allow himself to consider marrying into security and a life of ease. He renounces his desire with heroic self-restraint and remains firmly wedded to the Church and to his hard, Christian duty, offering Jane a life of servitude as an instrument in his work.

Charlotte is increasingly interested in such a character, a curate like several she has known, a good man who uses his virtue as a cudgel on those around him, as a means of distinguishing himself from them. He wishes to control Jane, too, to have her follow him to India as a missionary, a fate that would probably kill her. Beneath his quiet, controlled exterior he hides a fever of feelings, but he has no love for her. Jane must choose between love without marriage or marriage without love.

Charlotte cannot see a way out of this dilemma.

CHAPTER TWENTY-ONE

Decision

*E*mily walks through the kitchen and opens the back door. She understands Charlotte's hesitation. Outside, the light shimmers above the earth like a halo. The sun is like a balm on her skin. Her geese strut about proudly, glossy in the sunlight, and a flock of blue-and-pearl-necked black pigeons settle onto the ground. She breaks the roll from the breakfast table and scatters it, watching her eager, feathered vassals pecking happily. She looks up into the branches of the cherry tree and remembers climbing aloft, up and up, through the branches and leaves into the blue air, higher and higher, nearer to heaven, for the joy of it. She remembers, too, that moment of surprise, the tumble and fall, the sudden hard earth rising beneath her.

She is not entirely surprised by Newby's letter. She has always thought Charlotte's the weakest book of the three, though she has never said so, of course, and they have placed it first in their submission. There is not enough of Charlotte herself in the book. She has distanced herself too much from her text. Despite its title, she has not written about the real professor she loved. Much more of him is in Mr Rochester. Crimsworth is not sympathetic, a small man tortured by hypochondria and fear of death, who works his way through life with little enjoyment.

Emily has liked *Agnes Grey* ever since hearing Anne read passages aloud. Her younger sister has written so frankly, so scathingly, and so precisely about her experiences as a governess and her love affair with her father's curate, the good young man, Celia Amelia, as they called him, who has died so young. Who could doubt the sincere, hopeful voice of youthful indignation that expresses all Anne's opprobrium for the families where she has worked for so little regard?

Emily goes back inside and sits down beside Anne, who adores her, who followed her around as a child, when they made up the kingdom of Gondal together. She is wearing the grey-figured silk frock she has made herself with such difficulty, and her clear face is lit up with this good news. Emily wants her to have this joy in her life.

She knows, as she takes up the letter, rereads this publisher's words of praise, that her own book is the strongest and the most original. The other publishers who have turned it down and her sisters in their critiques have called its passions too brutal, its people too crude and violent, their natures too relentless and implacable. No one, Charlotte has warned, will want to read something so disturbing and dreary. Why portray such a dark vision of life? She should use more art and less intuition.

They were wrong.

Surely cruelty and endurance are inherent in nature and not inconsistent with the beauty of its vision. Has she not had to beat with her fists even her own dog, who walks at her side, to stop him from leaving his muddy fur on the beds?

With art she has made it all credible. She has structured her book cleverly using double narrators: first Lockwood, a refined man of means and education, removed from the excess of love, who looks on Heathcliff's world with a stranger's eyes; then Nelly Dean, the eminently respectable housekeeper, the practical woman, who knows the story from the inside as only a servant can do.

Heathcliff and Catherine will live on precisely because of their excesses. She knows she has taken risks and ventured into wild territory. She will gladly expand her book from the one volume into two. She already knows how to do this: she will add another generation. Newby has had the good sense to appreciate her secret strength. She will rework the time sequence to get it quite right for him. She will accept his offer.

She has reproduced events in the lives of those in her own family and of those she has learned about through the local gossips. She has described the places she knows so well: the interiors, the beloved landscape with all its savage beauty, its waste of heath, its wild sheep, its silence. She has written about property, money, position, and the power they give, which will anchor her book in reality. She knows firsthand the dangers of losing ancestral land to a usurper, the cuckoo in the nest, the dark-skinned gypsy, the wild vision that is part of her and that risks destroying her. She has written about the deep bonds of two lonely, feral children: a dark-skinned orphan boy and a bright girl, both left free to explore the wild land around them and their wild hearts within. She has rendered the passion of childhood on the page.

CHAPTER TWENTY-TWO

Anne

Charlotte says she will help with the breakfast dishes. She rises from the table, turns her face away, and leaves her two sisters to compose their letter alone. She goes into the kitchen to help the elderly servant.

Anne watches her go. She hears Charlotte say, 'I'll do this. You sit down. You shouldn't be on your feet with such a bad leg.'

'Poor Charlotte, what will she do now?' Anne whispers to Emily, who does not respond. Anne imagines Charlotte helping their old servant, who cannot see the potato eyes to peel them anymore. Anne sighs, but she cannot help feeling happy.

All her life, as the youngest child of six, Aunt's little pet, surrounded by her family's protective love, she has been made to feel helpless and dependent – a little nothing in her brilliant brother's eyes. Living at home, taught by Aunt and her older sisters and occasionally her father, she had little intercourse with the wider world, apart from a few tea parties with sheep farmers or the tradespeople of the vicinity, before she went out, first as a student to Roe Head and then as a governess. Yet she has always watched people closely, just as she watches Emily now, pushing her hair back from her face and writing this important letter for both of them without hesitation, pressing down hard on her pen.

What a complex person this sister is, someone whom Anne has never entirely understood, part of whom has always escaped her. Yet Anne has often felt she understood more than both her older sisters, or even her brother, about human nature. Being the youngest, one learns to watch, to copy, to adapt, and to say what will please. One becomes the messenger between the older children, the diplomat.

'If we make any money, we must share it with her,' Anne adds.

'Of course we will,' Emily says.

Anne feels generous, gracious, giving. She loves the whole world, especially her eldest sister, the one who has not been chosen, but she avoids her joyless, sensible face.

She looks around the small dining room, at the empty fireplace, the rocking chair, the dark sofa where black-and-white Flossy lies, the sunlight coming in the window and lighting up the leaves of the geraniums in the windowsill, and she thinks she has the right to a little happiness. She has worked so hard to try to give an honest description of the life of a governess: the hard work, the humiliation, and the miserable conditions she has had to bear for all these years.

Teaching is surely the most trying, the most humiliating, of occupations when pupils have no respect for their teacher.

She has been able to overcome her natural repugnance and shame in that position. She has left this home, these beloved sisters, and confronted her ungrateful pupils year after year, trying to maintain her dignity and belief in her own integrity. All her hopes for love and happiness with the man she adored have been lost. She fears she will never have the joy of marriage, will never be able to educate children, as she would have known how to if she had been given the authority to protect them from the harms of alcohol and drugs, as her brother never was. But she will have the satisfaction of seeing her small book in print and knowing that someone will read her words – some other poor young woman, perhaps, some-one sent out as she has been, alone, friendless, and put upon, who will know she is not entirely alone.

Why did the man she loved have to die so young? She wishes she could share her good fortune with her father's young curate. She sees him sitting across from her pew in the church, feels his gaze on her, sees his bright smile, hears his sunny voice. There was a lightness, a playfulness, a joy about him. She sees Emily at the piano playing Schubert Lieder while he sang, leaning toward her, his tenor voice sweet and caressing. She had not imagined that she would react to his death as she has. Sometimes she has moments of forget-fulness, almost as though he had never entered her life, and sometimes of anger, and then a memory will return like this with violence.

Would he ever have declared his love? How she had waited

for him to come to her that summer at Scarborough. But in her book she has written that scene on the beach. She has described the burst of violet-blue, the glinting breakers, the sea mews sporting above. She has rendered the sun-dazzled moment when her heroine sees him walking toward her across the sand in the early morning light. She has had the satisfaction of making the beloved curate arrive unexpectedly, of transforming her dreams into reality on the page. She has given her readers, too, that joy and hope. Now they will have her words in print forever.

CHAPTER TWENTY-THREE

Conflagration

Anne can hear her brother's groans and stumbling footsteps on the stone stairs. He is coming down slowly and staggering into the dining room, his hand hovering over his half-closed eyes. 'The light!' he moans. 'Close the shutters! Help me,' he begs. Anne puts a cautionary hand on her sister's arm. Emily immediately folds the letter she is writing, as well as the one they have received, and slips them into her book. She raises her eyebrows at Anne, who gets up to help their brother into the room, the dogs sniffing around him. He leans on her shoulder and seems to sink. He sits down, resting his head on Emily's shoulder. Anne fulfills his request, and the sunlit room is suddenly dim. The dogs slink into the corner, wary.

Their brother knows nothing about this publishing venture. How could they tell him? Proud and audacious beyond his station, he had puffed himself up with dreams of glory and had accomplished so little. Besides, he no longer has any discretion. They have all feared he might blurt out, in one of his drunken fits, their *noms de plume*, which are so important to preserving their anonymity. She looks down at him as he leans his body against Emily, lolling on her shoulder, while she brushes his hair back from his face and strokes his forehead. With his stained shirt, wrinkled trousers, bare feet, and wild hair, he knows so little about them.

Anne picks up the book with the letters and slips it onto her lap as she sits down. She cannot help wondering what he would do if he were to find out that she, the little nothing, has been offered a contract for her first novel. For a moment she is tempted to blurt it out, to crow, to confront him with the reality of his wasted life, the wreck of his talent, the ruin of his promise, the terrible suffering he has brought to all of them.

He sits before her with his head in his hands and asks where his father has gone. 'I'm afraid I gave the poor old man another bad night,' he says with a half grin. She says that while he was sleeping soundly, their father went out early. She turns her gaze away from her brother, his mass of unkempt red hair floating wildly about his gaunt forehead, his hollow cheeks and sunken eyes. He looks so thin he seems to be wearing someone else's clothes.

Emily comes in with a tray with the coffee, a glass of new milk, a toasted oatcake, butter. 'Come, drink the milk while it is still warm – eat. You must eat something, darlingheart,' she says, and puts her hand on his shoulder, concern in her gaze. He has probably not eaten for days, lying on his bed upstairs, but he says he does not want anything to eat, pushing away the tempting plate, lifting the cup of black coffee to his lips with a trembling hand. He complains of a headache, a wild din in his head, strange noises. 'I hear a constant buzzing. You cannot imagine the night I have passed. Horrible things flash before my eyes,' he complains, and stares at them with the frightened expression of a child. Emily takes the tray back into the kitchen, leaving Anne with her brother.

As Charlotte comes back into the room and sits down opposite him, he lifts his head, wiping a thread of saliva from his chin with the back of his hand. She cannot contemplate this piteous countenance without ire. How can he come downstairs in such disarray? Surely he could brush his hair, wash his face! He speaks of a dream he had. She does not ask him what it was, but turns her gaze away. But he insists, 'I must tell you my dream. I must speak to you! Charlotte, please!'

'Very well. Proceed,' she says stiffly, trying to be fair, kind, her mind on her book. She can no longer feel anything for him. She looks at Anne's calm face and neat figure instead.

'You were swimming in the beck, and there was a shark following you, and I just stood by and watched. Oh, I'm so afraid,' he blurts out, looking around the room, as though he sees something foreboding there. He leans toward her, clutching at her arm and lowering his voice to a hoarse whisper. 'Please help me. You must understand. I don't have anything. I have to get some money.'

She looks at his thin, anxious figure with horror. He smiles back at her mechanically, using his ancient charm on her, squeezing her arm. She remembers how he used these tactics with her aunt, stroking her plump arms, complimenting her coiffure.

Looking again into his mad eyes, feeling him clutching desperately at her flesh, she feels the affinity she has always felt, one that now makes her reject him. She detaches his hand from her arm. She cannot help him. She fights against the tightening in her throat. She must save herself. She must finish her new book, particularly now that her first book has been rejected once again. She turns away from him.

'Look at me!' he says. 'How can you turn your face away!' She does as he asks. She looks at him coldly, calmly, letting her eyes speak for her. She recalls her own hurt feelings, walking in the garden with her professor, her hand on his arm. She remembers how she longed to walk by his side forever; indeed, she still longs for his presence. She pictures the waves of his sable hair, the pride of his deportment, his indifference to his appearance. She remembers how she took to walking the streets of Brussels hour after hour, desperate, life's quiet stream broken up into whirl and eddy. How she dreaded going back to the dormitory alone, to the lugubrious dreams that came to her thick and fast. She was full of apprehension. The world seemed filled with messages in some secret code, as Branwell's is. All sense of purpose had dissolved. She walked all the way to the grave of dear young Martha T., her friend who had died of the cholera and been buried in the foreign soil of the Belgian hills. She stood there, weeping for all she had lost: her dead friend, her dead sisters, her dissolute brother, her home so far away, her teacher's friendship, intimacy.

As Branwell sits slobbering and chattering inanely before her, a moment she had put out of her mind, so strange had it seemed, comes to her. During that period of daily walking she had entered a Catholic church, St Gudule. Light came in aslant through the stained-glass windows, as it does now in the dining room at Haworth. The candles flickered in the gloom. She fell onto her knees in a pew, overcome with a sudden longing for human contact. Like her poor brother, she was driven by loneliness, guilt, and a need for intimacy. She wanted to tell everything, to confess. She was driven into a popish church to speak to someone about her unholy desire, to share the hate in her heart.

What was she thinking? Was she really ready to convert to her Master's church, to go back to her grandmother's religion, to be part of something ancient and lost? Did she not say every Sunday, 'I believe in one Catholic and apostolic church?'

She had watched as a penitent confessed through the grating, the voice whispering on and on. Then, in the immense half darkness, she dared to approach. The grating opened, and the priest inclined his ear. She was speechless. What was she supposed to say? She told him she was not a Catholic and did not know the rites of confession. What she needed was what Branwell wants from her, to absorb something, anything, from him, a Catholic priest!

At first, he had refused to hear her. 'My child, I do not have the right to bestow upon you the blessing of confession.'

'But I must speak! You must hear what I have to say!' she said with such conviction that the man was moved to say, 'My child, you are in serious trouble of some kind?' She spoke of the strange fever in her blood, calling it a kind of moral madness. She confessed that she was losing all that was good in herself and all that was human. Only animal rage – a passion stronger than any religious feeling, a desire to destroy, a hatefulness, remained.

'You have committed a terrible crime?' the priest had asked her in a worried tone.

'Only one of the heart,' she had said.

But nothing helped her. Indeed, she has not forgotten those feelings. As she sits at the table with Anne and her mad-eyed brother, she summons up for her book the madness of the wife confined to the attic. It is Branwell's madness and also her own. Bertha, the foreigner, the woman from afar, comes close to her now, possessed with the desire to hurt, to destroy, and with the preternatural ingenuity and energy to carry out her hateful desires. When she sees Grace Poole sleeping her gin-sodden sleep, she steals her keys and frees herself, roaming restlessly at midnight through the long corridor, going into the chamber of her rival, the young governess she instinctively hates, kindling the drapes of the bed, just as Branwell's bed had been consumed.

Fire will consume Thornfield and Bertha Rochester, as it might have consumed their parsonage and her brother if Emily had not rescued him. It is Jane who will have to rescue Mr Rochester as she, Charlotte, rescued their father, becoming his lifeline, changing places with him.

As she looks at her brother, another idea comes to her for her book. Clearly Mr Rochester must return, altered, someone to whom Jane now can go and remain blameless. He must call out to her just at the moment when St John proposes to Jane, when she is on the cusp of going to India as a missionary with him, which will surely bring her fragile life to its end. But Jane must go back to Mr Rochester and return to her past. She must go to the blinded man she loves above all others, the man who was there at the start.

Charlotte remembers an evening when she walked with her Master alone in the garden, the sky a soft pink. She can still hear him telling her they could communicate from afar through thoughts alone, reaching each other across time and space. His words are engraved in her heart. Did they not indeed speak to each other so often with a look or a gesture? Mr Rochester will call out to his Jane. Diminished, he will summon her in her mind. Yes, yes, of course, she sees it all now clearly: blinded and a widower, no longer threatening or frightening, he will summon her to his side, calling out, 'Jane! Jane! Jane!' as her father had done in Manchester in his great distress.

Jane will sit on Mr Rochester's knee as she, Charlotte, would have loved to sit on her father's knee as a child and brush his hair back from his brow. Jane will lie beside Mr Rochester, as Charlotte did beside her poor father, to warm his cold flesh.

Fire and air. There will be a great conflagration. Fire will come to Thornfield, prepared earlier, when Jane rescued Mr Rochester from his bed, a fire lit again by his mad wife in her glorious moment of freedom, going on all fours like a wild animal escaping from its cage, roaming through the narrow, low-ceilinged passageways of the upper story of Thornfield, going past all those rows of closed black doors, just as Jane herself has done in moments of restlessness, walking back and forth in the silence and solitude of the place, just as Charlotte's mind has freed itself in the writing of this book. The mad wife, laughing in her demonic, mirthless way, will descend the stairs to set fire to the room that had been the governess's, but Jane will no longer be there. She, too, will have escaped the confinement of Thornfield, escaped her position of dependency and subjugation. It will be the mad wife, Charlotte's own craziness, that will perish in the torching of Thornfield.

CHAPTER TWENTY-FOUR

Thorp Green

Anne watches Charlotte rise. She says she has work to do. She must go back to her book. She will write the last chapters. She leaves the room, walking with her head high, a strange glow in her cheeks. Her face is lit up with a joyous expression, almost as though she were going to meet a lover.

Anne thinks of the gay, insouciant presence of Celia Amelia, as they called the young curate she loved. She sees him coming into the room with a bunch of wildflowers in one hand and a valentine for her in the other.

But it is Emily who comes in, followed by Keeper. She takes up a mutilated ear, the result of many battles, and pulls at it absently while the big dog slobbers with affection, his head on her knee. She says tenderly to her brother, 'There is nothing to fear here, dear. You are among those who love you.' She leans her head against his, her dark brown hair half-concealing his cheek, looking at her brother with gentle eyes.

What can Anne say? At the time of the Thorp Green debacle she was determined to save him, as she would have a wounded deer or a fox caught in a trap. 'Perhaps,' she had said, 'the R.'s might engage Branwell to tutor Edmund.' And, with her recommendation – 'a brilliant mind: a painter, a musician, a poet!' she had told them, quite truthfully, after all – they had.

Ah! The arrogance of such a belief in her own power, she thinks now, this poor spectacle before her. His position as a tutor in the family where she was governess, though beneath him in so many ways, had seemed the best they could do for him. At least it was honest labour for a decent salary, and certainly a much better one than the R.'s had ever given her. And he needed the money so badly, as Aunt, unlike the three girls, had left him nothing in her will.

Anne was delighted to have Edmund, the R.'s spoiled boy, off her hands, though certainly her motivation was not a selfish one. She was so proud to be the one to come up with something that could help her brother.

Still, she had hard work to convince him to accept the post. She had pointed out the difference between their salaries. Mr R., though she despised his narrow mind, his hypocrisy, was not a skinflint. Perhaps he had allowed himself to be persuaded by Mrs R., who could be generous and liked to play the role of lady bountiful. Her brother was lucky to get double what they paid her, Anne thinks as she looks at him sitting slumped opposite her.

'We have work to do, my dear,' Emily finally says, then rises and disengages his hand. 'Come on, Anne.' The dogs get up and follow her as she turns to go out of the room.

'Don't leave me alone, please!' the brother cries out and grasps Anne's hand, but she rises too – what else can she do? She is afraid he will ask her again for money, which she cannot give him. Besides, they will need money to pay this publisher. She disengages her hand slowly and turns her back on him, but she looks over her shoulder at her brother, who watches them go with frightened eyes.

In her eagerness to convince her brother to accept the position, she had stressed the advantages. 'You'll have time to read, to write, to play the piano,' she remembers saying, truthfully, foolishly. Indeed, he had had far too much time with only the one boy to tutor, and that only in the mornings, while she was busy all day with the two girls. He had had time to dream his crazy dreams.

She had described the stately portico, the French windows, the eight lodging rooms on the first floor and nine on the second, the pianoforte, so superior to their own, which he would be allowed to play, the mahogany chairs. She had even expatiated on the moreen window curtains, the stabling of fourteen horses, the bidet and the bedstead imported from France. She was conscious of appealing to his snobbery, gushing over the eleven acres of pleasure grounds and paddock, the five servants, even the delicious cream and butter from the dairy, the beer from their own brewery.

Perhaps what had finally convinced him was the romantic tale of the Abbot of the Fountains, Jean de Ripon, who had died in the Monks House, where her brother was to be lodged, a timbered and wattled building that might have come out of a book by their beloved author, Walter Scott. Within sight of its gabled windows was still preserved the monks' circular stew pond, where fish were kept. Hearing this, he had said proudly, 'If I have to be an employee, I'd rather be employed by the aristocracy.'

She tried to tell him of their employers' faults during the voyage, speeding toward York in the new railroad from Leeds. Her words could not have been worse chosen. Instead of inclining him to caution, they must have led him astray.

'Tell me more about the R.'s,' he had urged. Ruefully she thinks of him now, putting his hand on her arm, blue eyes sparkling with curiosity and hope. His sisters had made him new shirts for this start, and he was smartly turned out. She had so much hoped to lead him into the path of righteousness.

At first she had deferred but, when pressed, she had added that Mr R. was an arrogant man, a landowner of considerable wealth who had in his library many books of sermons, including those of Carus Wilson, the director of Cowan Bridge, with their fiery Calvinist view of hellfire and damnation that Charlotte describes in her new book. Mr R. was of the Evangelical persuasion. 'He's obviously convinced his wealth and prosperity are signs of God's grace,' she had said with a smile and added, 'He's often engaged in an attempt to convert the heathen,' with a sideways glance at her brother. He had laughed.

She had added, 'He spends more time shut up in his study

with his sermons than with his own boy, poor little Edmund.'
What ideas must have already sprung to her brother's fertile
mind?

She told him Mrs R. was somewhat proud and arrogant
herself. She was a woman who, for her age, was too showy
in her attire. Still, she was a handsome woman and no fool.
'She's a good businesswoman and runs her domain
efficiently,' Anne told her brother. In Anne's opinion she was
more intelligent than her short-tempered spouse. She liked to
lie on a daybed and be read to – though she had a taste for
light literature. Above all a sentimental woman, she fancied
herself in the role of a victim. As was often the case, she was
not particularly sensitive to the feelings of others, but unfortunately Anne had thought it wiser to keep that to herself.

She did tell him how the mother doted on her honey-
headed Edmund, whom she, Anne, had been unable to teach
anything, let alone the Latin he should have acquired by
eleven. He was supposed to have been sent away to school,
but his departure had been deferred repeatedly. Unfortunately, none of the children seemed to have acquired even the
mother's taste for light reading. The girls were more
interested in boys or horses. The boy could hardly read a line
without help. She wasn't even certain he knew his alphabet.
'A wild colt,' she remembers saying.

None of this information seemed to distress her brother.
He smiled at her with that old belief in his genius. 'Chief
Genii Branii to the rescue,' he had laughed, using the name
from their childhood games and waving an arm in the air, as
though calling up his troops. He said he would know how to

take a boy of that kind in hand. And, indeed, he had, he had, for a while.

She could see how he was already transforming this information into some Gothic romance. Only she had not realized to what point he might be capable of losing touch with reality. She had watched him looking out the train window dreaming, as it continued onward, taking him to his doom.

Perhaps it would have made no difference what she had said. Certainly, he soon told her she was mistaken about the boy, who took to him with something like passion. The growing boy hovered beside him, not much shorter than he, his arm draped around his waist, his blond head turned up to smile at him mischievously. Her brother taught him songs, naughty rhymes, and allowed him to drink wine mixed with less and less water. He hardly kept him in the schoolroom – 'he'll learn more outdoors,' he would say when she remonstrated. He left the boy free, as her brother had been, to shout, to sing, to slam the door, to roam the land, sleeping wine-drunk, his mouth stained with berries through the summer afternoons in some shady spot, while her brother spouted his bad poetry to the bright air. One summer afternoon she had found them together, half-naked by a brook, the boy asleep, his damp curls like sunlight on the brother's pale chest.

Once she had watched them wrestling, grappling with each other, half in wrath, half in jest, until the boy fell to the earth, where he kicked him in the back viciously and then, when she was about to intervene, rubbed at the bruises lovingly.

From their first meeting, it was clear that Mrs R. would treat the tutor quite differently from the governess. He received no lengthy lectures on making himself likeable or on how to win over his charge. Indeed, he had no need. He gave in to all the boy's whims. Perhaps, at first, the mother's aim was simply to make sure her darling was treated with appropriate kindness. Very soon this may have turned into a real attraction. Her brother could be very attractive, capable of uttering the wittiest things, speaking gravely at times, his sentences taking fresh and unexpected turns. Anne, who so often felt unable to speak up, could not help being proud of her brother. Above all, he was capable of giving his interlocutor the impression that he or she was fascinating. Indeed, he found Mrs R. fascinating.

Anne, sitting upstairs in Emily's sitting room, sewing while her sister writes, can still see Mrs R.'s broad face suddenly lit up and laughing without restraint. Ah! Why had she not intervened? And how much was real and how much a figment of her brother's imagination?

Anne realizes now that she, too, vicariously, caught some of her brother's bright glow. She was permitted to grow closer to the girls, whom the mother increasingly ignored. She was even allowed to grow closer to their mother.

'I'm so glad you suggested your brother for the position,' Mrs R. said to Anne one morning, rustling into the school-room in a low-cut, pastel silk, bestrewn with ribands, a nosegay at her full bosom. Smelling of strong, sweet perfume, her cheeks flushed, she looked youthful, happy. She put her beringed hand on Anne's shoulder, leaned a little. 'He's the first tutor who has known how to take Edmund in hand. We are so happy to have him here.' She paused and added, 'Indeed, we are happy to have both of you here,' and she bent down and brushed Anne's cheek with her lips. What could Anne say? She wrote to her father, knowing the letter would be read aloud with pleasure to the whole family, that they were both much appreciated in their positions.

'You cannot imagine how kind she is to me,' Anne remembers her brother telling her one morning early as he rushed by her in the hall, his hair curled, blue eyes lit up, a bunch of wild, dew-wet bluebells in his hand, going into Mrs R.'s room. She had put her hand on his arm, leaned toward him, and whispered: 'Be careful, Brani,' but had he even heard? He had never listened to her, to anyone. He was being Northangerland, his invented character, inspired by Byron, and Byron's was the only voice he seems to have heard.

'How little she receives when so much should be accorded to her,' he whispered darkly to Anne, his eyes flashing with anger, as they both stood in the drawing room one evening before dinner and Mr R. paced back and forth in his black attire, looking aggravated and sombre at his lady's side, pontificating. It was increasingly clear that her brother was taking on the role of knight errant. But even then she had not realized that it would be Mrs R. who would seduce him.

For she had seen them together that morning early on the beach at Scarborough where the family summered. She loved to go there at dawn to walk in the freedom of the sand, the rocks, and the sea. There was never anyone there at that hour except for a few grooms airing their masters' horses, five or six riders, and a few elderly gentlemen walking for their health.

That morning, lifting her eyes in the dazzle of early light, she saw the gulls wheeling above and a man and a woman accompanied by a small black dog. At first she had not recognized them, but had only thought they were standing too close for people in a public place. Then she had noticed that the woman's hand was on the man's face, in an unmistakable gesture of tenderness, a caress, and she had seen the red of the young man's hair.

CHAPTER TWENTY-FIVE

Strife

*T*hrough the changing seasons of the year, Anne continues to watch her brother drift further into his own world. She works on her second novel, one about a woman tied to an increasingly degraded man, a woman who finally escapes her husband and comes with her child to inhabit a new place, a mysterious tenant with an unknown past, like Charlotte's Mr Rochester. She writes *The Tenant of Wildfell Hall* all through the winter and spring while extraordinary events occur in Charlotte's life.

Jane Eyre comes out before her own and Emily's books. Newby has asked for more work on *Wuthering Heights*, so that their books will not come out until December. *Jane Eyre* is published by George Smith to instant success, whereas their books are either ignored or compared unfavourably to their sister's. Anne tries not to read the reviews, not to think about them. She struggles to take pleasure in Charlotte's great success. She turns with determination to the writing and publishing of her second book for solace, hoping to do better this time, to write something with a wider canvas, something that will not be forgotten.

Now Charlotte holds another letter in her trembling hand. She looks flushed and cross. Recently, Charlotte has seemed so happy, delighted with one good review after another arriving in the post. Has her *Jane Eyre* not been called a 'book of decided power', 'one of the most powerful domestic romances', 'full of youthful vigour and imagination'? Her book has even had a great run in America.

Yet today Charlotte's hair, usually so neat, and the skirt of her grey muslin dress are in disarray. Her cheeks, often so pale, are flushed. She waves her new letter in the air at her sisters and announces in an irate tone, 'Your publisher, that shuffling scamp, is up to his old tricks! We have to put a stop to this! I don't know how you can continue to deal with this unscrupulous man! Why did you let him publish your new book, Anne?'

Anne puts down her sewing and looks across the room at Emily, who takes her feet from the fender and looks back at her. In this the two sisters have remained united. Newby, though he has delayed the process and though there were many errors in the text, has published both *Agnes Grey* and *Wuthering Heights*, as he has promised. He had taken a chance with their first books. *Wuthering Heights* has been called tasteless and shocking: 'Readers would be disgusted, almost sickened, by details of cruelty, inhumanity, and the most diabolical hate and vengeance.' Even when praised, it was mistakenly regarded as an early and artless book by the writer of *Jane Eyre*.

Despite, or perhaps even because of these reviews, the books have not sold badly. Newby, unscrupulous though he may be in the use of Charlotte's name and in publishing only two hundred and fifty instead of the promised three hundred and fifty books initially, has managed to promote the sales. So how could they not remain with him, who has even brought out a second edition of their books and has promised to publish both their second novels, despite all this storm of opprobrium? Of course Anne turned to him for her second book.

Emily comes forcefully to her younger sister's rescue. She draws herself up, puts one hand on her hip, and says, 'What do you mean? Newby gave Anne decent terms this time. She has already had fifty pounds from him. Her book is doing quite well, almost as well as your own, despite your recommendation not to bring it out.'

Charlotte stares at Emily with something like furor in her eyes. Anne presses her hands together and says a silent prayer: *God give us peace*. She looks around the small room and feels the lack of space. A close summer evening. She can hardly breathe. Often, these days, she is overcome with breathlessness, particularly at moments like this. She gets up and opens a window, breathes in the air. She can hear the church bells chiming the hour.

These days there has been increasing dissent among the sisters over the smallest of things. Anne and Emily are sometimes aligned stubbornly, bitterly, against Charlotte, clinging to their publisher; sometimes Emily, deeply hurt by the scathing criticism and incomprehension of her 'disagreeable' book, faces off against the others.

Anne notices Emily's pale face and belaboured breathing. She, too, breathes with difficulty and suffers perhaps even more from this constant and unfavourable comparison with her sister's book. Anne has seen the reviews Emily keeps in her desk, those that compare her book unfavourably to Charlotte's. The critics have not understood her.

Emily has told Anne she longs to escape this world, which she calls 'this shattered prison'. Anne cannot follow her there. Indeed, she has worked constantly to finish her second novel, refusing even to go out walking with her sisters. She has taken a certain satisfaction in being the first of the three to publish a second book, and with some success, albeit a scandalous one.

Now, as Emily lifts her head, she sits down beside her and gives her a grateful look, puts her hand on her arm.

Charlotte has told her youngest sister that her new book is just too close to the naked truth. 'You need to varnish, to soften, to conceal,' she counselled her, speaking of their brother's rapid descent almost to madness. But the public has perused with great interest the story of the drunken husband and his unfortunate wife, much of which came from her observation of her brother and her own experience at Thorp Green.

Charlotte says, 'If I can't say what I think to you two, to whom can I speak? I'm sorry to have to say this, but I still think the publication of that book a mistake. In any case, this is going too far. I have thought this over all day and I just feel I cannot stand by and do nothing with my publishers accusing me of dishonesty!'

'What has Mr Newby done now that displeases you so?' Anne asks. Charlotte comes to her, thrusts her letter from George Smith into her hands, and stands over her while she reads.

'Newby has told the American publishers your novel is the second written by the author of *Jane Eyre*. He maintains all our books have been written by the same person,' Charlotte tells them. She pulls out a chair and sits down at the dining room table beside Anne and turns to her. She puts a clenched fist on the table. Her nose looks large and red and her eyes flash as she adds, 'We have to do something about this. It's not fair to George Smith, who has been so correct in all his dealings with me. He had promised them my second book! I don't care if the public confuses our identities, but I can't have my publisher suffer.'

Anne looks at Charlotte's flushed cheeks and the harsh glitter in her eyes. Is this really what bothers her sister, or does she not want to be associated with their work? Is she afraid that the unfavourable reviews of their books will influence the reception of her own? Is she tired of their riding on the coat-tails of her *Jane Eyre*?

For a moment, Anne almost wishes none of them had ever written a book or certainly ever brought their words before the public. Is the game worth the candle?

Despite Charlotte's disapproval, Anne has been determined, indeed, felt it was her duty, difficult as it might be to render it, to warn her readers of all the dreadful consequences of inebriation. She needed to reach out to others who might be similarly afflicted. She laboured hard to reproduce truthfully and without recourse to sentimentality or obfuscation exactly what she has seen at close hand in the houses of the wealthy where she has worked: the swearing and brawling, the maudlin speeches, the boasting and blaspheming under the influence of drugs and drink.

She has wanted to warn the public, too, of allowing a child excessive freedom. She has tried to stress the necessity of bringing up a child, whatever his class or kind, with the sort of discipline that was essentially lacking in Branwell's life.

And is not her Huntingdon akin to Charlotte's Rochester? Still, she sees Charlotte's point and understands her ire.

'What are we to do?' Anne asks her older sisters, as she did the year before. She has no wish to antagonize Charlotte further.

Charlotte continues, 'This is just another example of your publisher's duplicity! It would have been much better to change houses.'

Anne looks across the room at Emily, who is smiling with a defiant coldness that alarms her. Charlotte says, 'We will have to straighten this out. This charge will have to be refuted. We will have to reveal our identity, tell George Smith who we are, that we are three – three sisters.'

Emily, who has been sitting very still, now rises and paces in her deliberate and energetic way. Hands behind her back, she is followed by her big dog, who pushes his head into her hand. Her eyes dark with anger, she says, 'We all promised never to reveal our identities. We understood that from the start. You cannot strip me of this essential cover! I could never have envisaged writing my book otherwise. First, you forced me to publish my very private poems, for an uncomprehending public. Now you want to expose me to the public. It is all very well for you, with your success, to step out of the shadows, but think about me. You know what the critics have already said about my book. What will they say if they discover it was written by a woman, the daughter of a country parson? Have the kindness to leave me out of this.'

'But everyone thinks our books were written by one person – and that is not true!' Charlotte says.

'What does it matter what the world thinks? We know the truth. When we are dead will be soon enough for everyone to find out,' Emily says, turning on her heels and staring fiercely at Charlotte.

'But I cannot do this to my publishers,' Charlotte replies firmly, looking up at Emily. 'It is a practical matter. You must understand that. It's also a question of my integrity.' She adds, 'Besides, there have been other sources of confusion I would like to clear up.'

Anne cannot deny her eldest sister's reasoning. She says, 'She is right about this, Emily. Charlotte and I should go immediately up to London to see her publishers and sort this out. There is no other way.'

'As you wish,' Emily says, eyeing Anne coldly. She turns toward Charlotte and adds, 'If you are going ahead with this, you should first tell Papa. Let him read *Jane Eyre*. Let him into the secret, before all the others. Let him share your success.'

'Read him some of the good reviews you've had,' Anne urges Charlotte. 'He will surely be very proud.'

CHAPTER TWENTY-SIX

✧

Rapprochement

She will tell her father about her book, Charlotte thinks, if not about theirs. Though a few reviewers have attacked her 'coarseness, lack of femininity', these reviews seem only to have spurred the sales. Her only sadness is that her sisters' books have been compared so unfavourably to her own.

The letter that gave her more pleasure than all the good reviews together came from the great Thackeray, the living author she admires most. When she dedicated the second edition to him, she discovered why he had sat up all night reading her book: she has told his story of a mad wife shut away, a husband tied reluctantly to this burden. This is a coincidence that has worked in her favour. Perhaps fame is always a series of circumstances of this kind.

But now people are saying that she was a governess in his household and the model for his Becky Sharp in *Vanity Fair*. She will have to step out of the shadows of her anonymity.

She will have to declare her gender, her name, at least to her publishers, if not to the world at large.

She will always be grateful to George Smith. *The Professor*, though he had rejected it, elicited such a kind letter from him that she had almost preferred it to a cursory acceptance. He asked if she had anything else in hand. Indeed, she told him, a three-volume work, almost finished. Then she had completed *Jane Eyre*, spurred on by these encouraging words and the thought that a receptive publisher was waiting to read it.

She has given her readers a happy but believable ending: 'Reader, I married him,' she has written. Mr Rochester, damaged by the inhabitant of the upper floor at Thornfield, as her father has been by his son, is not the man he was. She has described a happy marriage, one where Edward Rochester, going to consult an eminent oculist, gradually recovers his sight. He is now able to find his way without being led by her hand. Like her father, he can see the sky again, the hills around him, and his darling boy, who has inherited the colour of his eyes.

She has ended her book with an account of the curate, St John, who has continued resolutely along the way he has chosen as soldier in the army of the Church. 'Firm, faithful, and devoted; full of energy and zeal and truth, he labours for his race,' she has written about the man Jane refused to marry, who is dying in India while she lives on happily with her Edward at Ferndean in England. She has taken her revenge on all the narrow-minded, self-absorbed, and self-righteous curates in her life, who have used religion as a way of controlling others, of proving they are better than the rest.

Yet, prophetically, she has given him the last word. She ends her book with St John's words, which are also the last in the Bible, from the Book of Revelation, 'My Master,' he says, 'has forewarned me. Daily he announces more distinctly, – "Surely I come quickly!" and hourly, I more eagerly respond, "Amen; even so come, Lord Jesus!" '

Thanks to this book, she has reached the large public she has always dreamed she might reach. When Anne asked her if she was surprised by this success, she told her she was not entirely surprised. The emotions she has felt writing this book have been such that she felt her readers, too, would experience them.

She will let her father know that all those hours she sat writing by his side in the half dark in Manchester and the days she worked on her return to Haworth have not been in vain. She fears her father might hear of it from another source. Were he to read this book, would he not recognize parts of his daughter's life, perhaps even different facets of himself in its pages? She must be the one to take off the mask, to speak up and declare her identity.

'I'll tell him after dinner,' she tells her sisters.

But she stands before the door of his study for a long moment with her book in her hands. What if it were to anger him? Can she really step out of the shadows of her childhood, her deference to him, and admit she has written not just the light poetry that he has done himself or even a novelette like his own *Maid of Killarney*, which he might have condoned, but this book that has been both acclaimed and denounced as shocking, coarse, anti-Christian, and anti-establishment? Can she own these words, which speak of the longings of a woman for fulfillment, for love, for the same rights as a man? How will her father, an eighteenth-century man, a parson from a backward Irish village, respond to such a cry for liberty and love from a woman, his daughter, the one who nursed him in the blindness she has reproduced in these pages?

Then she realizes that she will follow Anne's suggestion. She will have recourse to his snobbery, to his pride. She will read him the glowing reviews, where her work has been compared favourably to the great writers of the day. He will respond to the praise from the world of letters, if not to the words of her book.

She knocks on his study door, and awaits his summons to enter, holding her book behind her back, the best reviews folded in its pages. She finds him sitting at his writing table, bent over in the pool of light from the lamp, making notes in the margin of his *Modern Domestic Medicine* in his strong hand, crossing his t's widely, his two clay pipes and his spittoon before him. She is filled with pity at the sight of him straining his eyes, no doubt, to find some hope for his beloved son.

She approaches quietly and looks over his shoulder at the open page on *delirium tremens*, which he is studying with the help of his large magnifying glass. She is suddenly filled with rage. Is his only concern, then, still his boy? Why does the prodigal get the feast and not the dutiful child? She has always disliked this parable, felt its injustice. Her brother has always been her father's obsession, a sore he continues to lick at, as a dog would. He has never felt the same way about his dutiful girls, who have struggled so valiantly, have taken care of him and his household, and have suffered so painfully from their lungs. Why is he not studying a page on asthma, which afflicts poor Anne? Does he not hear her struggling to breathe all through the night?

'What is it?' he asks curtly, looking up at her. He has had another bad night with his boy, and his blue eyes are red-rimmed and bloodshot.

Again, she hesitates to bear news that may not bring him joy. Her success will only make his son's life seem more lamentable. Perhaps his own as well? He has sold few copies of his books. Since the death of his wife, he has not published a word. But now she cannot retreat. Also, she wants him to read this book. Her written words settle all accounts. She tells him she has been writing a book, and she would like him to read it. He responds without any apparent surprise, saying, 'I'm afraid the manuscript, my dear, would try my eyes.'

All that scribbling, he thinks. He remembers the scratching of the pencil in the dark, day after day, as he lay in that room in Manchester. Is this the product? He has been blinded like Saul and then regained his sight, but his eyes are still not strong. How can she expect him to read her illegible, cramped hand? He knows her tiny script discourages any perusal, indeed, was probably invented for that reason as a child. Why is she not content to show her sisters her work, as she usually does?

As if he didn't have enough on his mind with her brother begging him for money to spend on drink and drugs or wrestling with him in the night for the gun on the wall, so that he never knows which one of them will emerge alive in the morning to stumble down the stairs. Last night he had sat up until late in the parlour, his head in his hands, listening to the shouting and cries, the beating on the upstairs door, the screams coming from the locked bedroom where the boy had been confined upstairs. He thinks of it as a kind of madness that comes upon his son and takes him away from him. Suddenly he is elsewhere, this beloved boy, a stranger to him.

Charlotte protests and says that this book is not just a manuscript. It will not be difficult to read. It has been printed. She takes it from behind her back and lifts it up toward him, a gift.

'Printed!' he exclaims, appalled, putting down his magnifying glass. Now, he suspects, the girl has lost her mind, too. He had had such dreams once. But he has faced reality, curtailed his efforts. He has not tried to publish or even write anything for years apart from his letters, his weekly sermons – and even those are often composed on the spot.

He has suspected that his poor girls were trying to publish something from time to time. What is this mania for fame and glory in his family? Why can they not, as good Christian women, accept their poverty, their insignificance, as their mother did? What folly! Who would be interested in their words? Still, he knew that there had been letters sent off from the parsonage and packages received. He saw the brown paper with its many addresses, one after the other crossed out. Poor, misguided girls – who did they think would publish their work?

He recalls a time when the postman had asked him about a Currer Bell, for whom so many letters had arrived – a pseudonym, he presumes. He wonders why they chose that name and hopes it has nothing to do with his Irish curate, Arthur Bell Nicholls, a good man, perhaps, but poor and undistinguished and certainly not good enough for any of his daughters.

He is not as blind or as foolish as they might think, though he has said nothing about it, not wanting to embarrass his girls. He presumes that after many failures and heaven knows how many rejections, this one must have finally resorted to paying some dishonest publisher a small fortune to have her words appear in print. What vanity!

For who would want to read something by an obscure parson's daughter, living in a remote region of Yorkshire? And what could she have written about? What can she possibly know, having lived so much of her life alone, sheltered, protected in his cramped parsonage, with nothing around her but barren moors, her spinster sisters, her spinster aunt, and an elderly, ignorant servant, a delinquent brother, a parson father – pray God she has not written about him! She has lived all her life either at home, at girls' schools, or as a governess with small children, shut up in various nurseries like a nun. What does she know about the human heart, about love?

If he admits it, he has often found the prattle of his girls tiresome, even this sensible girl by his side who has looked after him so devotedly. Light verse, he can imagine her writing, as he has done himself, after all: for the edification of young people, for children. But this is apparently a book of some length. He squints with suspicion at the thing.

She lifts it higher, thrusts it at him. 'Read it, Papa, please,' she says, and stares at him, her eyes, he is afraid, filling with tears. He is obliged to take the heavy thing into his hands. So many pages! He looks at the cover, the frontispiece, turns the page to the dedication. The girl has even dared to dedicate this book to the great Thackeray!

'The expense! But just think of the expense, my poor dear!' he says. Has she spent her aunt's entire legacy? Borrowed from her sisters? What must this have cost? Twenty-five, perhaps even fifty pounds? When they are all struggling to survive! Money that should have been saved for her later years, when he will not be there to provide a roof over her head! What foolishness!

The girl protests, saying she must read him a few reviews so that he may realize how profitable this venture has been. She has not lost money, but rather gained some – indeed, much more than she has ever had, a sum she would never have dreamed of. She lowers her gaze and shyly mentions a sum that he cannot imagine receiving: five hundred pounds.

'Good heavens, what would you, as a woman, want with so much money?' he asks her. She is now in a position to offer him a few luxuries, to make his life easier, she says, carried away, no doubt. She is dreaming of carpets, curtains, perhaps even pictures, more shelves for their books, she says. She will be able to do what her heroine does in her book for her cousins, refurbish the parsonage. How strange that she has described something that will become true.

He sighs at what he imagines must be her confusion – she has never been practical or had much sense of practical things – and says, 'Reviews?', for who on earth would have reviewed this girl's book? Still, as she seems determined and has several in her hands that appear to be printed, he tells her to go ahead. She draws up a chair, sits down beside him, adjusts the lamp to shine on her pages, and commences to read in her clear voice.

❦

She has decided to begin with one of the shorter ones, something that goes quickly to the point:

'Decidedly the best novel of the season: one, moreover, from the natural tone pervading the narrative, and the originality and freshness of its style, possessing the merit so rarely met with nowadays in works of this kind, of amply repaying a second perusal. Whoever may be the author, we hope to see more such books from his pen.' She stops there and looks up at her father, who is staring back at her. 'Good heavens, child, what did you do for this gentleman to have him write something of the sort?' he asks.

She reads another as response, from *The Era*, 'an extraordinary book. Although a work of fiction, it is no mere novel, for there is nothing but nature and truth about it. A unique story, for we have no high life glorified, caricatured or libelled; nor low life elevated to an enviable state of bliss. The tale is one of the heart, and the working out of a moral through the natural affections.'

She cannot resist reading him one more, which has pleased her particularly and which refers to the voice in the book: 'It is soul speaking to soul; it is an utterance from the depths of a struggling, suffering, much-enduring spirit: *suspiria de profundis!*'

Her father looks at her now, his mouth slightly open. He says, 'Leave the book with me, child, and we'll see what we will see.'

VOLUME THREE

London
1848–53

CHAPTER TWENTY-SEVEN

Smith

Anne packs a small box with a change of clothes for herself and Charlotte, which they send on ahead of them. Emily does not even say goodbye as they prepare to set out on foot for Keighley after tea. When deeply moved, she is often silent and remote. She practises loneliness like a sport. Standing in the hall, Anne watches her climb the stairs slowly, a hand to her side. She thinks of Byron's lines: 'From my youth / My spirit walked not with the souls of men / Nor look'd upon the earth with human eyes.' How can they leave her like this? Such sombreness and restraint frighten Anne.

Emily stands for a moment on the stairs in her grey dress and half-turns toward her sisters in the hall, her face suddenly caught by the light from the window. A woman with hanging hair, a smile set on her lips, a smile of suffering. 'Emily!' Anne calls, wishing she would at least say goodbye, wish them a good voyage, but she does not answer, just lifts her hand slightly toward her shoulder. She continues up the stairs, closes the door behind her, and goes into her small room alone, with the bunch of foxgloves Anne picked for her that morning in a glass by her bed, her notebook with her beautiful poems, her big dog. Anne would like to call her back, but how?

Charlotte says, 'We must go, or we'll miss our train,' and she is obliged to follow. Branwell is out somewhere, hunting down money, or at the Old Cock in Halifax, where he has run up a large bill.

They set out on foot to walk the four miles to Keighley. Charlotte strides ahead down the path and, almost running, Anne follows her in her printed cotton dress, her narrow shoes, her bonnet. A late-born lamb crosses her path as it runs bleating up the bank to join its mother.

Escaping the house, the trouble at home, bent on proving her own identity, she is suddenly filled with determination, despite the ominous clouds in the low sky. How low it hangs in these parts, a place of everlasting rain.

Despite a thunderstorm and heavy rain that soaks them both, their thin muslin dresses clinging to their skin, they keep going along the narrow path, leaning forward, heads lowered into the rain and wind, with a sense of purpose. She will tell the publishers who they are. She will set the record straight. She is not ashamed of anything she has written. On the contrary, she has done her best to describe the world as she has seen it. She has refused to compromise. Let the critics know she is a woman. Let them judge her accordingly. Why should a woman not be allowed to speak up?

They take the train and get to Leeds just in time to take the night train to London. They shiver in their damp clothes, but they are in first class for this venture, thanks to Charlotte's newfound fortune.

※

They arrive in the early morning at Euston station and step out of the train onto the platform. The skies have cleared, the day is bright, the light harsh in their startled eyes. They go to the only place they know, the one where Charlotte stayed with Emily before going to Belgium, where their father had stayed before them, the Chapter Coffee House.

Charlotte steps out of the carriage into the street, with its noises and smells of early morning. Somehow, despite her fatigue and sensitivity to noise, all this bustle – the horses' hooves on the cobblestones, the cries of vendors, someone shouting out something from a window – reassures her. The city with its business, its rush and roar, all the earnestness of people getting a living, excites her deeply. She is proud to be a part of it.

'Look,' she says to Anne as they are ushered into their low-ceilinged, dingy room, and Anne is hunting for something to give to the porter who has brought their bags, 'St Paul's'. She points out the spire, which they can see from the small window. The hum of the bells in their colossal, dark-blue dome feels like a summons to freedom.

She remembers her first visit to this inn, with Emily, before her trip to Belgium. Little did she realize at the time that she was about to undergo what has perhaps been the definitive emotional experience of her life. Now she feels her spirit shake its half-fettered wings free.

At the familiar and reassuring sight, she suggests they eat something and rest a while before going to confront Mr Smith. It does not occur to her that, this being a Saturday, he might not be at his place of work. Exhaustion and anxiety over their voyage have made her hungry. They tidy up and head into the restaurant, a long, low room upstairs. They sit opposite each other at a table by the window. There is the hum of conversation, the clatter of china and cutlery. A waitress drops a knife to the floor.

Recklessly, Charlotte orders without considering the price of the items. 'I'm famished,' she says. Besides, for the first time in her life she has money she has earned by her own wits. What a thrill to think that she is not as dependent on her father as she was in the past. Here they are in London. She feels a lift in her spirits. She looks around the room and out the window at the buildings and the street below. *All of this is mine, mine, mine! Thanks be to God.* She lowers her head and mumbles a prayer. *For what we are about to receive may we be truly thankful.*

They order eggs and haddock with buttered toast. They eat the large breakfast in the dim, pannelled dining room almost in silence. Charlotte watches Anne eat with great pleasure. Her little sister seems to be enjoying their joint venture. How few voyages, how little pleasure she has had in her life! How hard they have worked! They smile at each other across the table, chewing, with sudden complicity. They have come this far together.

'I'm so glad you came with me,' Charlotte says, and watches Anne wipe the grease from her mouth with her napkin. She says, 'Poor, dear Emily. I wish she had come with us.' Charlotte grasps Anne's hand. She remembers the nurse with her large lamb bone and her bare feet, and smiles: Humber. Perhaps she is with her three little girls, whom she spoke of so fondly. Perhaps she has even read *Jane Eyre*.

When she has eaten, Charlotte says, 'I must lie down for a moment,' overcome with exhaustion. They go to their small room, with its double bed. They remove their bonnets and shoes and close the shutters. She lies down by Anne's side in the darkened room, as she once did beside her father in Manchester. She is almost asleep when Anne rouses her, touching her arm. 'Ought we to go now?' she asks nervously. She rises and walks up and down the room.

'Yes, it's time,' Charlotte replies. They do their best with their crumpled attire, wash their faces, tidy their hair, slap their cheeks to bring forth a little colour, bite their lips, and put on clean gloves.

Charlotte stares at her face in the mirror. Will George Smith believe she is the author of the book that has set all of London talking? She can hardly believe herself that she has written this book, which has made Currer Bell famous. She believes almost that Currer Bell has nothing to do with Charlotte Brontë, that this book has come from some other, mysterious source. But she has George Smith's letter and money as her proof, carefully folded in her reticule.

Do I dare go in and tell George Smith I am the one who

has written this book? How can she give up her anonymity, the androgynous name that has freed her to write this? Can she say, 'Reader, my name is Charlotte Brontë and I am the author of *Jane Eyre*'? She remembers that moment in the dark room in Manchester catching a glimpse of a face in the mirror and wondering who it was.

Now she must face the world, or at least her publishers. She must expose herself to strangers. Will they think her an impostor, not sufficiently learned or sufficiently grand?

They set out, venturing into the busy, confusing streets. They are surrounded by noise, bustle, strange city smells: London on a bright Saturday morning. People glance at their crumpled country clothes. In the glare, Charlotte already feels exposed. She thinks of sitting in the half dark and silence of her father's room, the name of her heroine coming to her out of thin air as she straightened her father's sheet. In a way she would prefer to be back there at his side, writing her book in the safe quiet. She clutches at Anne's arm, glad to have her steady sister beside her with her good English face.

In the excitement and strangeness of it all, they get lost trying to find Cornhill Street. Eventually, Anne spots it. Now Charlotte hesitates, standing outside what seems to be a large bookstore. She thinks of Emily shutting the door on them, her closed and weary face, of Branwell sitting slumped over his glass of spirits, of her father coming into the room and telling her sisters she has written a book rather better than he had expected. Anne hovers beside her, seemingly similarly overcome with misgivings. 'Perhaps we should just go home,' she suggests. There are tears in her blue eyes.

But Charlotte takes Anne's arm and says, 'Come, we have come all this way. We must go in.' They enter the cool shadows of the bookstore, where young men mill around busily, ignoring them. They go up to the high counter and approach a young clerk. He peers down at them from over the top of his glasses, looking somewhat suspicious at their appearance. Charlotte is suddenly uncomfortably aware of her dowdy dress, now creased, and of her bonnet with its brim bent, having suffered in the rain.

When the clerk inquires what he can do for them, in a tone implying they have no business being in this place, Charlotte speaks in such a low voice that he cannot hear what she says. When asked to speak up, she raises her voice, which now sounds horribly loud to her, and asks to see Mr Smith. The clerk asks for their names. Charlotte looks at Anne, who shakes her head and then declines to give the information. She cannot bring herself to tell this stranger who they are. They are told to wait in a tone that is not encouraging.

They wander around looking at the books, many of which have been sent to her by this publisher. She picks up Darwin's *Journal of Researches in Geology and Natural History of the Various Countries Visited by H. M. S. Beagle*; a book with illustrations of South African zoology; Ruskin's *Modern Painters*. She wonders if they will ever be ushered into Smith's illustrious presence or will have to languish here ignominiously ignored, while the many young men and boys bustle around them, for the rest of the day. She is aware that their insignificant appearance, their out-of-date country dresses, and their refusal to give a name must not hasten the process.

George Smith is busy dictating a letter to a clerk when he is told that two ladies are waiting for him. 'Who are they?' he asks. Despite his youth – twenty-four years old – he is exhausted, having been up early to come to work this Saturday morning. He frequently works twenty hours a day, having inherited his father's business two years before. Money has been embezzled, his father's affairs are in disarray, and he is obliged to provide for his mother and four younger siblings. Today he has been working since seven. He is hungry, too, not having had time for anything but the cup of tea his mother gave him at dawn. He thinks of the mutton chop that she likes to provide for her hungry son on his return home, with a cup of green tea. His stomach rumbles ominously. And now some unknown women have come to see him in the middle of the morning, while he is busy with a letter concerning his complicated affairs in India.

He suggests that the clerk tell them to return some other day, but the polite young man looks rather worried and says the women have already been waiting for a long while, and he suspects by their country clothes that they have come some distance to see Mr Smith. 'I wouldn't be surprised if they had taken a night train,' he says.

'Goodness me,' Mr Smith says, and hopes they don't have some dog-eared manuscript up their sleeves, something that has happened to him before. He sighs, 'All right, then, bring them in. I'll dispatch of them fast.'

The two women come in the door and stand timidly, side by side, not venturing into the room. Neither of them is young or pretty, and certainly their clothes are out of date. He is about to tell them he is a very busy man when one of them approaches and hands him a letter, which he can see is in his own hand. He looks at it and realizes it is one he has written to his best-selling author Currer Bell, who has all of London buzzing with discussions on whether the author is a man or a woman and whether the three books that came out under the name Bell were written by one or several men, or perhaps even by a woman.

He looks at the diminutive woman and asks rather sharply how she came by the letter and why she now returns it. Has she stolen it, or merely found it in the gutter? What does she hope to gain by bringing it to him? Is this some sort of blackmail? He looks at her in the clear morning light of his sunny office and sees something like a grin on her face, a flash of amusement in what he now realizes behind the glasses are large, intelligent eyes.

'You sent it to me—' she says with a little laugh, putting her hand to her breast for emphasis.

Can this be, is it possible that this little woman is the author of *Jane Eyre*? The woman motions to her sister and adds, 'We are three sisters, you see.' George Smith stares at her, taking in the tiny hands, which she waves delicately in the air, the glow of the hair and skin.

'You are the author of *Jane Eyre*?' he gasps. 'You?' He

stares at her, taking her in for himself and also, he is aware, for posterity. He is already writing his memoirs, an account of this meeting, noticing the head that seems too big for the little body, the uneven teeth. He wants to know all about her figure, her dress, her tiny, narrow shoes. He wants to touch her, feel if she is real. This small, frail person, hardly five feet tall, with these dainty hands and feet, has written a large, strong book that has already made him a great deal of money.

'Yes,' she says in a voice that is bell-like, like the name she has assumed. 'Yes, I am.'

'Goodness! Great goodness!' he says. He claps his hands, announcing,'We will have to have a dinner party! We will have to introduce you to all of London! My mother and sisters will be delighted. Wait until they see you! Wait until Mr Thackeray hears about this!'

CHAPTER TWENTY-EIGHT

✿

Opera

Charlotte declines this invitation to be shown off to the famous *literati* of London but accepts one to go to the opera that night, under yet another pseudonym. She and Anne will be the Misses Brown. Despite a headache and in her plain, high-collared country attire, she goes up the crimson, carpeted steps, up and up, at the Royal Opera House, surrounded by a throng of chattering, laughing, elegantly dressed people. Like the ladies and gentlemen in her own and her brother's stories from long ago or someone in a fairy tale, she goes through the throng on the arm of her youthful and fine-faced publisher. Despite her unease she glances up shyly at his creamy complexion, his dark, close-trimmed side whiskers, and – what pleases her most – his cleft chin.

Her first impression of him was not particularly favour-able. He had looked her up and down so carefully, staring at her under the bright light of the skylight in his office, rather like a fishwife eyeing a fish to determine its freshness. Now, his large, dark eyes glance at her face quickly and then scan the crowd. With buoyant step he walks beside her, in his full evening dress. He talks fast in his mellow voice, makes little jokes, waves his white-gloved hands in the air, rather like a magician who has conjured this all up just for her, her personal Prospero. He is attempting good-naturedly to put her at ease. Beside him trip his two tall sisters in their low-cut taffetas and ribands, and cruising ahead, rather like a stately ship, his serene and portly mother goes on with ponderous step.

Though Charlotte is aware of the supercilious stares and the puzzlement and disconcertedness of his mother and sisters, she is amused by the contrast between her modest appearance and George Smith's studied politeness. She has made him a lot of money, and he cannot wait, she suspects, to tell the world the secret, that he has on his arm the author of the celebrated *Jane Eyre*, that this little plain woman at his side has written the big book they are all talking about.

They enter a box near the stage where they have excellent seats. Despite her protests, Mr Smith insists that she and her sister sit in the front row.

'I want you to be able to see it all: both the stage and the audience,' he whispers in her ear. So they sit bolt upright on either side of his formidable mother in her mauve dress, her tortoiseshell spectacles tucked into a fold at her considerable bosom. Mr Smith, flanked by his tall sisters, sits in the row behind like a pale flower.

His mother turns to the older sister, the one who wears spectacles, and peers at the playbill shortsightedly. She says, 'We are so glad you could both come with us this evening, my dear,' but she wonders why on earth her son has asked these two plain country creatures to accompany them to the opera. She calculates how much the excellent seats in the box he has taken for all of them must have cost. What extravagance! Surely the firm, though it is going from strength to strength under her son's expert guidance, is not doing so well as to afford this? Why has he gone to such trouble and expense?

Indeed, she would not have come out this evening at all had her son not insisted. He had rushed home late, looking flustered, excited, his cheeks uncustomarily flushed. He refused to eat any dinner, not even the tempting thick mutton chop she had had the servants prepare for him. 'You should eat, George, otherwise you might faint,' she said.

Instead, he had said breathlessly, 'There is someone I very much want you to meet, Mama.' When she had pleaded fatigue, he added, 'It is very important to me – well, to all of us – you will see,' with a little mysterious smile. He had ordered the carriage, told them to dress for the opera, and set off with them to collect the mysterious guests.

He hinted at some secret he had promised to keep, which led her to expect something else entirely: a great beauty, perhaps, or a great fortune, or a celebrated writer he was about to publish, someone brilliant and amusing, perhaps even the great Thackeray himself. Instead, there are these two subdued and plain creatures, who are acting now rather like two children at a birthday party.

She smiles at the younger one, who is the prettier of the two, with her fair hair and blue eyes. She has something vulnerable and appealing about her, but surely her son is not interested in either of these women romantically? They must be in their early thirties. Obviously two impecunious women, in their ill-fitting dresses, considerably older than her son, with a certain distinction of manner and a shyness bordering on haughtiness – she will give them that, but of the faded variety. They look like proud governesses, the sort of put-upon ones of whom lively children would take advantage.

'You must excuse us, for we are not used to such pleasures in our hill-village home,' one of the Misses Brown – if that is really her name – says and smiles at her. Mrs Smith notices the fine eyes behind the spectacles, with their odd, slightly superior, amused gaze. What is it that amuses her so? And what is her source of superiority?

'Is it your first visit to London, my dear?' she asks. She doesn't remember where George said the women come from, some small, bleak place in the North.

'No, no. We have been here before.'

'And when were you last here, may I ask, Miss Brown?'

'Actually, six years ago, en route to Brussels, where we – I went to school.'

'You did? You must speak very good French, then.'

'Quite,' the woman says without false modesty, smoothing the folds of her dress. Mrs Smith notices the small hands, the neat, well-polished nails. There is a pregnant silence. Something about this woman, a certain reticence, intrigues Mrs Smith. She has the impression she could tell her something interesting if she wanted to. Does she have some secret accomplishment? Is she even wellborn? The voice is sweet, but is there some lingering trace of Irish or Scottish accent?

'And you stayed at the same place in London?' Mrs Smith asks, as they have picked the two women up on Paternoster Row at the Chapter Coffee House, such an odd place, surely, with its low ceilings and dingy rooms, for two gentlewomen to reside.

'Yes, that is where my father stayed when he first came to London,' she says, and looks back with her unflinching gaze.

'I have never been in that part of London before, I must confess,' Mrs Smith cannot help but say with a little smile.

The woman looks her in the eye and says, 'No, I suppose you wouldn't have.'

She would like to question the women further, but now the orchestra is playing the overture, the curtain is rising on the first act, and she can only watch the two of them with their rapt expressions. She notices, too, how her son passes the elder one his opera glasses assiduously, so that she can see every detail.

Mrs Smith watches the two sisters rather more closely than she does the Rossini. She wonders if they have ever been to an opera before. They seem totally absorbed. George has said they will be introduced as country cousins, but obviously they must be otherwise. The family has no cousins up North. The headache, mentioned earlier, seems forgotten.

Mrs Smith finds the Rossini performance an ordinary one. The Barber of Seville was never one of her favourites. She prefers Verdi, and her stays are uncomfortable. She battles with her *embonpoint* but cannot resist sweet things. She would have preferred to remain home this evening, without her corset, in her comfortable peignoir, nibbling on a few *petits fours* or a box of chocolates, but she has always found it hard to resist her handsome, clever son, who has been such a help to her. Why has he insisted on her presence this evening? What does he wish her to do for these women?

Surely this must be a business arrangement. In matters of business, Mrs Smith has entire confidence in her enterprising son, young as he is. He has always been her favourite, she thinks, turning back to smile at him in the shadows behind her and to squeeze his hand and raise her eyebrows with a glance of complicity. *You see how good I'm being, making polite conversation with these two poor women, all for you, my dear.*

It seems such a short while since he was a boy. In the shadows of the box and with a Rossini aria in the air and these two strangers at her side, she sees him again in the short grey pants of his school uniform. How she worried about him, such a thin boy, and delicate – she was always concerned about his health and his heart. She couldn't bear to think of how he was teased by his classmates, and he fainted at the slightest pretext. Yet he has always had a strong will, a stout heart, and such determination. He has done as he pleased, even getting himself expelled from school at fourteen and insisting on joining the firm. He preferred working with his father, and they had given in to his wishes. Yet he has always responded to her when she has called upon him. Her dear girls seem faded and pale beside him now, even in their bright best dresses and posies.

Since her beloved husband's illness and death four years ago, she has had to rely increasingly on him. He has proven to be such a zealous, hard worker with an excellent business sense, which his father, unfortunately, good man that he was, did not possess. What would she and the rest of her children have done without her enterprising son?

It is he who has sorted out that dreadful imbroglio with the unscrupulous partner she had warned her husband about, but he was too good-natured to understand. Her son, though he seems so innocent, has his practical and prudent side. But she finds him this evening to be behaving in a most peculiar manner.

During the interval he jumps up and offers to go and look for refreshments, should anyone so desire, though the women demur. They are not women used to being waited upon, she deduces, more and more puzzled.

She turns from them to her son, but for once he does not seem to hear what she is saying. He turns the conversation onto general topics, the delights of London, the museums they will surely enjoy, the parks, even the zoo, obviously trying to amuse these women, to detain them in London, or at least to draw them into a dialogue. They seem almost struck dumb and look rather pale and piqued. She wonders how healthy they are. She hopes that this performance will not be repeated, but is very much afraid she may have to entertain them the next day for Sunday lunch, which will be quite an ordeal. She wonders what her beloved boy has in mind. Business is all, she fervently hopes.

~

Sitting in the box with Anne next to this handsome, middle-aged mother in her mauve dress, Charlotte is reminded of how she and Emily first met Madame H. on the rue d'Isabelle. She remembers their arrival and warm welcome, the elegant room, all the bric-a-brac on the mantelpiece, Madame Parent and her exciting tales of the French Revolution, and how they sat side by side on the white sofa and shook Monsieur H.'s hand. How she still longs for her Master! And how she had disliked him at first sight! Her black beetle. How wrong she was, too, in her first estimation of his wife.

Her first impressions are not to be relied upon. Still, she cannot help feeling drawn to this woman who sits so solidly at her side in the shadows of the box. She prefers her to the prudent, half-Scottish son, who seems rather calculating. She likes the mother's lively brown eyes, her clear cheek, the way she offered her warm hand so promptly on greeting her. She likes her decided bearing, her strong profile seen in the half light of the opera box. A handsome woman and certainly, this evening, all amiability, all graciousness. She likes the way she scolds her son jokingly, takes him to task as though he were still a boy, the way he calls her 'Old Lady'. There is obviously a close bond of affection and trust between this mother and the young, promising son that moves Charlotte. She prefers him as a son and brother.

She wonders what her own life would have been if her mother had not died when she was so young, if she had had the support and unconditional love of an intelligent woman, someone who could have guided her through the complexities of life, who would have tempered her father's self-absorption, controlled his explosions of wrath. She thinks of her mother's letters, which her father has recently allowed her to read, letters of such tenderness, frankness, and humour, they moved her to tears. How different her life would have been with someone of that kind at her side to encourage and exhort.

She takes in all the gestures, the complicit glances between this mother and son with a little stab of sadness. Never will a woman, even her good friends from school, her dearest sisters, treat her thus. She wonders what role, if any, this woman will play in her life.

Before the Smiths leave them at the Chapter Coffee House, they insist that they come the next day for lunch at their home.

CHAPTER TWENTY-NINE

·❦·

Fame

George Smith writes her many lively letters, on Charlotte's return to Haworth. These sustain her in the writing of *Shirley*, her next book, where she tries to bring her beloved sister, Emily, back to life. These letters and her visits to London enable her to continue with her work, despite the family tragedies that now occur one after the other, like the beads in a dark necklace of woe: first Branwell, then very quickly Emily, as though she could not live without him, and then dearest, dearest Anne. Charlotte is left alone with her father.

Now she longs to escape the parsonage, the cold and empty rooms, despite the bright new curtains and carpets she has been able to provide. In her grief and solitude, with only her poor lonely father, she wishes to get away, to abandon the old man who clings to her.

Above all she would like to share what she has written

with her dead sisters, as they had so often done, night after night, walking together around the dining room table arm in arm, the three of them telling stories, encouraging, criticizing, laughing in the freedom of the dark, their long intimacy, their father's absence. How she misses them! Above all she misses the laughter, the shared language of childhood, the little private jokes. She is seized with a great lassitude. She wants to laugh at herself and at others.

When she allows herself to escape her duty as a daughter, her father's presence, she travels to London, trips that have to be made alone and with only her self-absorbed father to recount her adventures to on her return. When she comes home there is no one to listen attentively and with such lively interest, living these visits vicariously as Emily once did, though she would never come with her. Now Charlotte moves through her life of fame alone, only her ailing father – his ailments seem to occur when she is about to leave – and her dear friend from school, Ellen N., for love and support.

Still, she forces herself to continue with the business of everyday life, even finding a new dressmaker, thanks to her friend, buying a bonnet with a pink lining. Like her Jane before her abortive wedding, Charlotte buys a flurry of new clothes, which are trimmed with fur for special occasions. In a desperate attempt, she augments her thin hair with a false plait around the crown.

There are dinners at the Smiths' house, visits to galleries, lectures, the Crystal Palace, the theatre, and even the zoo. She receives a complimentary ticket from the secretary of the Zoological Society and writes to her father about the amazing animals there. She has seen some frogs that are almost as big as Flossy.

There are meetings with important people, with the aristocracy, with the Scottish essayist, philosopher, and historian Thomas Carlyle. There is even a meeting with the great Thackeray, who disappoints and provokes her ire by introducing her to his mother as 'Jane Eyre'. How dare he! Does he not understand the difference between imagination and reality?

Invited to stay in the Smiths' fine home, she is given the best guest bedroom. When she enters the large, calm room she feels she has dived down into some precious chamber in the sea, as she used to imagine when making up stories with her brother. With its pale green walls and counterpane, the lined cream curtains rising and falling in the air, the dressing table with the triple mirror and its frilled organdy skirt, the big bowl of cut flowers, the wax candles on the mantelpiece, the fire kept burning day and night, she feels herself to be in a haven of peace and voluptuousness. The wide four-poster bed with its diaphanous hangings looks like a ship about to sail. She throws herself across the bed and stretches out luxuriously.

She is even assigned a personal maid, who is willing to help her undress and manage her hair if she so desires, and who will even bring up her meals if she does not have the courage or the energy to go downstairs and face a room full of guests. She can choose to lie at her ease with a book or sit up at the writing table and correct her proofs.

Sometimes Mrs Smith knocks on the door, having carried up the tray herself, bringing some delicious dish she has ordered especially for her. 'May I come in?' she says, peering round the door, coming and sitting on the bed beside her and chatting in her comfortable way. 'You must bear up, my dear. You must not give way to despair. Your work is so important to us, to everyone.' She speaks and pats her on the cheek. Charlotte feels spoiled, watched over, cosseted, for the first time in her life.

Sitting at the fine dining table decked with silver, delicious dishes, and peonies mixed with lilac, below a brilliant candelabra and on the left of a white-haired, distinguished member of the aristocracy who is making desperate attempts to draw her into the conversation, she remembers her wretched days as a teacher at Roe Head and as a governess. Here she is the one who sits, half-listening to the man at her side who is trying to impress her with an idea for a book he is attempting to write – 'If I only had the time, I'm convinced I could do it,' he says.

'Perhaps,' she says, looking at him.

She remembers the large number of ladies and gentlemen sprawled on the velvet sofas of the grand house or sauntering about in the park, coming and going bewilderingly, or presiding in the evening at the dining table in their black ties, jewelry, and décolletés. When the gaze of one of them happened to fall on her as she walked against the walls, it seemed he or she saw nothing, less than nothing.

She recalls that first dreadful breakfast with the small children who would not sit in their seats and how rudely they shouted at her: 'You are a servant and stupid!' How she was spurned and looked down upon. How rude the children were to her.

Here, George's younger sisters and brother are extremely polite. They bring flowers for her room, curtsy, and shake her hand. The youngest, a pretty little girl who has taken a particular liking to her, takes her gently by the hand and asks her to read to her from a favourite book.

When Charlotte rises from the table and goes into the drawing room, all eyes turn to her, not so much with admiration but with interest. They stare at her with curiosity. Some of them appear embarrassed. They notice her in her grey-pink dress, the light in her smoothly coiffed hair. She enjoys this attention in a shameless, childish way she cannot remember feeling since she was a girl. There is something exquisite at being wondered about.

She spots the children's governess, the *Fraulein*, sitting shyly with her sewing in the shadows of an alcove. She makes a point of singling her out, sitting next to her, and talking to her at length, remembering her wretched days in that position. 'You must miss your home,' she says. 'Do you have brothers and sisters?' she asks with longing. 'Tell me about them.' But she is not left on her own with the *Fraulein* for long. Because of her *Jane Eyre*, everyone has come to the dinner to converse with her. They seek her out. It is she who has to put at ease the young, pretty woman in a pink dress who has come up to her and is stammering and shaking before her. 'Your book was so b-b-b-beautiful,' she tells her. 'I felt as if I was reading my own story.'

'What a lovely thing to say. How kind of you,' she says.

Her tastes are now consulted; her opinions on all sorts of odd questions are suddenly of value; she is treated as a precious and rather fragile thing. People want to find out who she really is. They want to know the facts behind her book, whether the school is based on a real one, whether someone as good as Helen Burns or as bad as Mr Brocklehurst really existed. What they really want to know is whether she has written her own story into her novel; how much of it is true? How could she answer such a question? She doesn't know the answer herself. Yet her own life, the tragic deaths of her sisters and her brother at such young ages, seems to interest people perhaps as much as her book.

Even with these polite people around her, who try to please, with her obliging young publisher and his welcoming mother hovering near, she cannot help but hear her brother's final prayers, her father's final cries for him, and the unexpected last word that came forth from her brother's lips: 'Amen'.

He had been ill for so long, so debilitated by his drunkenness, they had not realized the end was near. Yet a change had come over him as he neared his demise; he seemed suddenly filled with all the affection he had once felt for his family as a boy. She hears her father's inconsolable cry at the death of his only son, calling out like David for his Absalom, 'My son! My son!' She hears, too, her father's ardent pleas not to abandon him. When she fell ill after the death of this brother she had loved and admired so much as a girl, 'You must bear up for me!' her father said over and over again, as

213

he had when he lay in the dark room in Manchester.

She sees, too, her darling Emily, staggering down the stairs, a poor shadow in the last days of her life, insisting even then on fulfilling her household duties, feeding her Keeper, who followed her coffin and sat silently in the pew with the rest at her funeral and lay at her door waiting and howling, night after night. She has found Emily's last lines: 'No coward soul is mine, No trembler in the world's storm-troubled sphere; I see Heaven's glories shine, And faith shines equal, arming me from fear.'

She sees dear Anne, too, who, despite her firm faith in God, continued to hope for more time, valiant Anne who longed to do something good with her life and who in the end had asked to go back to the sea, to Scarborough. She hoped it might restore her, that she might be brought back to life in the place where she had spent a few happy moments and imagined an even happier moment for her Agnes Grey, who meets the curate she loves on the beach. It was a place where she sat at the window, the sun lighting up her face, looking across the bay, a place where she died with words of encouragement on her lips: 'Take courage, take courage, Charlotte.'

Charlotte tries to take courage, sitting here in the Smiths' grand drawing room, surrounded by these elegant people – *God give me courage to continue!* – but she cannot help feeling alone, almost as much in her fame as she had once felt in her anonymity as a poor governess in the families who mocked and tormented her. Then, at least, she could think of her sisters, her brother, write to them when she retreated alone to her room or store up in her mind details of her life to recount at Christmas. Now she has to be careful what she tells her father, presenting only what he would want to hear about her life.

How extraordinary and a little absurd it all seems, looking around the beautiful room at the company in their fine clothes. She is the same person, after all, yet suddenly here she is courted, praised, and flattered. Suddenly her life has become interesting to others because of *Jane Eyre*.

At the same time, she is aware that George Smith's mother, in her mauve dress – she seems to favour mauve – has her lively brown eyes on her, that she watches her closely with the same wariness as Madame H. did. Mrs Smith stays close beside her all through the dinner party, hovering, to see if she needs anything, she says, but at the same time watching her especially if there are men, especially her boy, at her side. She brings her a cup of coffee in the drawing room herself, which Charlotte refuses. Surely the woman can see she presents no threat? Surely the mother is aware of her integrity, her shyness in company, her pure morals?

She senses once again that she is being discussed. She is not even sure that someone has not gone through her things in her fine room, though perhaps it is only the maid who has pressed her dresses, washed her under-things, scented the folds of her gowns. She notices how the mother and son stop their whispering when she approaches them in the drawing room, and how they turn and lean closer to each other, sitting together on the sofa before the fireplace, when the guests have left.

CHAPTER THIRTY

Disappointment

The mother enters her son's bedroom to bring him his early morning tea and the newspaper herself.

'You shouldn't be up. It's too early,' he says sleepily, stretching out a hand toward her and reclining on his plump pillows as she wakes him, coming into the room crooning, 'Rise and shine, my boy.' She comes with the tray and sits beside him on his bed, smooths the embroidered linen sheets, pours the milk from the little silver pitcher, and drops in the sugar lumps, as she has done so often. As she stirs, round and round, she speaks to him in a low, dulcet voice. She says she knows it is early and he has much on his mind, but she needs to talk to him on a serious matter before he leaves for work.

'And what matter could that be, Old Lady?' he says playfully, turning her ring around her ring finger. She looks at him lovingly, shakes her head and strokes his hair back from his handsome forehead. She takes an indirect approach,

'Such a lovely person, so honest and well meaning, so serious, so earnest.'

He knows whom she is talking about, of course. He pulls himself up slightly in the bed against the plump pillows and nods his head. He adds, 'Such a gifted writer and an important one for us at the firm. She has brought in others, you realize: Thackeray and Elizabeth Gaskell, for example. I'm optimistic about the new book she's working on, too. From what I have read so far, it may well be her best.'

The mother says she understands that as an author, she needs to be courted to a certain extent. Certainly she has done her best to make the woman feel at home. Still, she goes on to voice the danger of too much intimacy with an earnest, intellectual woman of this kind. 'It's not so much the fact that she has no fortune to speak of, my dear – I wouldn't bring that up, you know well – or even that she is so much older than you and really quite plain. You must have noticed, well . . . the teeth! for one. Poor thing! All of this I might be able to overlook, indeed, would overlook, but what really terrifies me, my darling – and I have only your good at heart, you must know that – is that there is such a stain of illness in that family, my dear, both the sisters dying one after the other like that, not to speak of the dreadful brother, whom they say was quite mad, quite mad, you know,' the mother murmurs in a low voice.

'There's nothing of that kind to worry about, Old Lady, I assure you,' he says gaily, propping himself up further and pressing her plump fingers between both his hands. Then he takes the tea she has brought him as she always does in the mornings and drinks the cup down quickly. She adjusts a curl on his forehead lovingly. 'Be careful, my darling, be careful. You don't want to get yourself inadvertently into a compromising position,' she counsels as she leaves him to face his day.

❦

Still, the mother hears about the invitation to a trip up the Rhine and, more alarmingly, a project to pick up her youngest boy from boarding school in the Highlands of Scotland with the author. She will have to take the matter in hand.

She calls Charlotte into the blue drawing room. 'Come and sit near me, dear child,' she says, patting the silk-covered sofa. She looks her in the eye, takes her hand in both of hers, and says, 'I hear George has asked you to accompany him on his trip to the Highlands.' Charlotte nods without a word, just staring ahead with her rather small brown eyes. She does have pretty eyes, the mother will admit. She truly likes this woman, knows she is good, and admires her work, but the mother must protect her son at all costs. She looks at Charlotte directly, squeezes her hand between her own tenderly, leans toward her, and whispers, 'Surely, darling, you are not seriously considering going on your own to the Highlands with him? Think of what people might say! Would it not put you in a compromising situation?' She adds, when Charlotte apparently finds nothing to say in response, 'I'm only saying this because I am so very fond of you,' and puts her hand to Charlotte's cheek and gently lets her fingers tap her playfully. 'Think it over, my dear,' she adds.

In the end Charlotte does not go to the Highlands, but she does visit Edinburgh in romantic Scotland, the country of her beloved Scott. She visits Scott's monument and walks up to Arthur's seat in Holyrood Park with her publisher at her side. Here she finds George Smith at his best: with his fine figure, his youthful spirit, his good face, his even temper, his charm. There are moments of rare happiness, despite her recent losses. With this engaging, energetic man at her side, listening so attentively, bending his head toward her to listen to her responses, deferring to her, she forgets her own sorrows, her father anxiously waiting for her return. George Smith makes it clear that she is important to him, that he wants at least to divert her, to amuse her.

They visit the castle in Edinburgh and listen, fascinated, to the guide who tells tales of murder and points out what is thought to be the bloodstain from the body of the Catholic courtier, Rizzio, stabbed again and again as he tried to hide behind his queen.

They stand on a terrace overlooking the city. The mist clears and the sun shines through the cloud for a moment as she surveys the scene. She feels that she has invented it all, that the city belongs to her, to her with this young, attractive man at her side, her publisher, a man who, like her black swan, believes in her genius. She looks up at him and realizes that she half-believes this young, enterprising man might take her for his wife. She might move into the lovely house in London, with the mother and the son, make the pale-green bedroom all her own. She might have a new family with him. Does she not have the right to such happiness? Suddenly she remembers Madame H.'s warm baby in her arms, the nurse who spoke with such longing of her little girls.

But she leaves George Smith without any promise of marriage or words of love. She is obliged to retreat, breathless, exhausted, to the house of her friend, at Brookroyd near Leeds, where she lies in the guest room and dreams of the couchant crag lion she has seen in Edinburgh. She tells Ellen N. that Edinburgh is to London as a vivid page of history to a dull treatise on political economy. Ellen is left to nurse her in her fragile condition, while her father writes her letters from Haworth, working himself up into a state of extreme anxiety about her health and perhaps even more over her heart. He begs her to come home, insisting that the bracing air of Haworth will soon sweep away what he calls the dust, smoke, and impure malarial air of London.

Then, like Monsieur H., and with a sickening familiarity, the letters from George Smith taper off into trivialities. Waiting for his letters becomes almost unbearable, and she tells herself she would prefer to know that none will ever arrive. But she cannot stop herself from writing to him. She writes him to say that her ability to continue her work depends on his offering her some hope, however small, in return. She needs his friendship, at least, as she once needed Monsieur H.'s. She has mistaken the transitory rain-pool for a perennial spring.

Under his mother's indomitable pressure, her alarm, Charlotte presumes, he has given her up. She concludes that his interest in her was at best only in a valuable author who needed to be courted for a while.

All that remains is to transform him in her great book, *Villette*, into Graham Bretton, in order to oblige her publisher to read of himself described with all his emotional limitations, just as she obliged her father to read of his blindness in Mr Rochester. She recreates for his perusal and that of the world a man of limited passions, and no one besides his beloved mother can lay claim to them. The heroine turns to another, someone clearly modelled on her first passionate love, Monsieur H. In the end she writes the book for him, for the first person to discern her gift, her range, her brilliant verbal promise, with his observant eye, and in her heart she dedicates it to her Master with gratitude.

Finally, George Smith writes no more. He sends a smaller cheque than she has expected, a much smaller one than he pays certain of his authors.

She waits once again for letters, becoming increasingly depressed and finally ill when all that arrives from London is a simpering epistle from his dear Mama announcing, in a most circumlocutory way, his betrothal to another. She writes a letter of congratulation to George Smith:

My dear Sir,
In great happiness, as in great grief – words of
sympathy should be few. Accept my meed of
congratulations – and believe me,
Sincerely yours,
* Charlotte Brontë*

EPILOGUE

⚜

Haworth, Thursday, 29 June 1854

*B*efore breakfast she stands in the dim, early morning light in the little stone church, like her heroine, Jane Eyre, but with her father's curate, Arthur Bell Nicholls, at her side. In white embroidered muslin, head drooping like a snowdrop, she glances at him from under her pretty bonnet, trimmed with green leaves. Shyly, and with little hope of happiness, she looks at this tall, handsome, bearded man, part of whose name she has adopted once before.

She says the habitual words. No one protests or finds reasons to gainsay this marriage, not her father, who is not even present, certainly not her old teacher from Roe Head, who has come to stand by her.

At the last minute, already dressed in his wedding finery, her father has pulled out, collapsing into a chair with some imaginary complaint. He has fought this union fiercely from the start, coming up with all sorts of strong arguments. He has invented ailments for Mr Nicholls from which he has never suffered. In the end, though, he has lost the battle. It has occurred to Charlotte that men are full of petulant nonsense, and that their supposed strength is rather less than a girl's.

The wedding might never have taken place had not the old servant asked her father, within Charlotte's earshot, whether he wished to kill her by interfering with it. He has relented with the promise that the couple will live with him at the parsonage, that he will be taken care of until his death, and that he will not have to give his daughter away. He has found his curate unworthy of his now famous daughter's hand, though he comes from a much finer Irish family than his own peasant forebears.

But how could she refuse her Arthur, who remained so faithful at her side through so much tragedy? How could she refuse him, whom she found howling at the gate, begging her to give him some small shred of hope, who wrote her so many desperate letters, just like those she wrote to her teacher and her publisher? How she has recognized this passion, so much like her own had been! He was in love in the worst way: without reason, without pleasure, and without grace. How could she not pity him? She cannot but marry him, reader, despite her fears and misgivings and though her mind is on her ghosts, those absent ones who are ever present in her heart, dearer to her than life, who are buried in the church, her two elder sisters and her two younger ones, Emily and Anne, who went so fast, one six months after the other, following on her brother, who went so quickly before them.

Again, she recalls Anne's generous dying words and takes courage standing in the church by her new husband's side, glad of his support and love. She lets him take her hand, fold back her veil, and kiss her on her lips.

What she does not yet know, of course, is that this will be a surprisingly happy marriage, if all too brief, and that she and her Arthur will truly become of one flesh and one bone, as she has described in her masterpiece. They will travel together to Wales and Ireland, where she will be impressed by Arthur's distinguished family, by their home, Cuba House, and by his discretion and modesty.

Like Jane, she will realize that she is with child. She will not expect to die so soon. Within nine months of this wedding day, her father and her husband will stand together by her corpse. They will remain shackled together, as her father once was with her aunt. They will bury her in the same church.

She cannot know that her father will outlive her by six years, with the husband he never wanted for her, never respected. The indomitable old man will die at the age of eighty-four. God will continue to protect him from illness and bodily harm, as he had prayed that He would do. He will spend his days alone, shut up in the silence of his study, with his medical dictionary and his clay pipes. *Thy will be done on earth as it is in heaven. Forgive us our trespasses as we forgive those who have trespassed against us. Lead us not into temptation.*

In the long darkness of his dreary nights, he will lie awake, straining to hear his children's footsteps, as he has heard them so often, walking round and round the dining room table, making up their stories, speaking them aloud into the dark, laughing, hushing one another for fear of waking him, their voices rising up the stairs as they come to him. 'Hush, you will wake Papa,' he will hear them say in his mind. He will lie awake in the dark and strain to hear the sound of their voices, or even the thump of old Flossy's tail on the stone floor. He will think he hears the sound of a pencil scratching.

ACKNOWLEDGEMENTS

Though this book is a novel and its characters fictive, I remain indebted to the great Brontë biographers, Gaskell, Gérin, and Gordon, and to the many others who have written on the Brontës, as well as the Brontës' letters, reviews, and, of course, their books, from which I have quoted freely.

The spark for this novel came from a line in Lyndall Gordon's biography of Charlotte Brontë: 'What happened as she sat with Papa in that darkened room in Boundary Street remains in shadow.' I have tried to imagine what might have happened during the writing of *Jane Eyre* in Manchester and Haworth, and how the book changed the lives of the Brontës and all the rest of us.

I am also, as always, grateful to my three beloved girls, Sasha, Cybele, and Brett, who have read my work over the years with such attention and love; to my agent of many years and many books, Robin Straus; to my friend Marnie Mueller; to my colleagues at Princeton and Bennington, and particularly to Joyce Carol Oates for her encouragement and support; and to my editor at Viking Penguin, Kathryn Court, for her vision and good judgement; and to Katherine Telischak.

A CONVERSATION WITH SHEILA KOHLER

Of the biographies that you used in your research, which would you recommend to readers looking for more information on the life of Charlotte Brontë? Beyond Jane Eyre, *which of the Brontës' novels would you recommend to a reader wanting to become more familiar with the sisters' work?*

I would particularly recommend Lyndall Gordon's *Charlotte Brontë: A Passionate Life*, which was really the inspiration for my book, as well as *The Life of Charlotte Brontë*, Elizabeth Gaskell's classic biography. As for the Brontës' novels, *Villette* is one of my great favourites, such a modern novel it seems to me, where Charlotte Brontë describes the loneliness of her life in Belgium with poignancy.

Wuthering Heights, too, is a great favourite of mine and such a beautiful description of the passions of childhood. I would also recommend the lesser known *Agnes Grey* by the youngest Brontë girl. It is a precise and sensitive description of the life of a governess, the humiliations and trials of a young woman in love.

Why did you decide to write a fictional account of the lives of the Brontë family? Do you feel a particular kinship to Charlotte Brontë or any of the other Brontë sisters?

As Fritz von Hardenberg has said, 'Novels arise out of the shortcomings of history.' The line in Lyndall Gordon's book, 'What happened as she sat with Papa in that darkened room in Boundary Street remains in shadow,' inspired me to imagine what might have happened when Charlotte sat by her father's bedside in the dark and began to write her great book.

Like many woman, I believe, I do feel a special bond with the Brontë girls. In my case an aunt (there were three sisters and one boy in my mother's family) read to my sister, an older girl cousin, and me the first chapter of *Jane Eyre* shortly after my father had died. I was seven years old and the description of Jane's experience in the Red Room, where she thinks she sees the ghost of her uncle, made a deep and lasting impression on me. It was perhaps the spark for this book, which starts with a father and daughter in that darkened room.

I also have a daughter, Sasha Troyan, who writes novels, and I am interested in how these pursuits and talents run in families, particularly families of girls. I have three girls of my own: a writer, a painter, and a history professor, and I often share my work with them as the Brontë girls did. Each one of them has been of great help to me with my work.

How long did the research for the novel take? Were there moments in writing the book where your creative impulse went in one direction and the truth of Charlotte Brontë's life went in the other? Which did you follow?

J. M. Coetzee once said to me when I told him about my project: 'Don't stay too close to the truth.' I think that it is good advice. Certainly, one cannot falsify the facts that are so well known, and I hope I have never done that. However, there is so much one doesn't know about someone else's life, even someone so famous, and there I let my imagination work freely. Besides, there is always a selection of facts made. I was particularly interested in the bond between Charlotte and her married professor and also in the relationship between these three sisters, who died so young. My own very dear sister was killed in her thirties and I still miss her. Perhaps writing this book was a way of reaching out to her.

It's hard to give an exact time for the research of this book: like so many women, I have been reading the Brontës since I was very young – seven, as I said, and I read *Villette* as a teenager in boarding school and was moved by the feverish atmosphere of that book, too. I read a great number of biographies, of course, and found the letters of the Brontës particularly helpful. While I was writing the book, I went to Haworth with one of my daughters, and we walked together across those moors under a threatening sky. It seemed essential to me to see the parsonage and those low grey skies to understand the lives of these amazing women.

In your acknowledgements, you mention Elizabeth Gaskell as one of Charlotte Brontë's biographers, but she's also mentioned within the novel as one of George Smith's other authors. Can you tell us a little about her life and how her work influenced your writing?

Elizabeth Gaskell was, of course, Charlotte Brontë's first biographer and a close friend, and a writer in her own right. Though her biography, perhaps, stresses Charlotte's saintly side a little too much for the modern reader (she wanted to refute the Victorian accusations of coarseness), it is still a wonderfully sympathetic and informative biography. I think I was particularly influenced by her not altogether favourable portrait of the father. Since then he has had much more positive press, but I felt some elements of her initial portrait were probably valid or valid for the character in my book.

What power did writing provide Charlotte Brontë? What was the prevailing attitude toward women writers? Were there any other means for women to achieve status/independence or a sense of equality in the nineteenth century?

Writing eventually brought Charlotte Brontë fame and recognition after years of struggle and humiliation as a governess and teacher. Certainly Robert Southey, the poet laureate, considered writing a man's domain and told Charlotte so in no uncertain terms in his famous letter to her. Many of the women writers of the time felt obliged to choose pseudonyms that hid their sex: George Eliot is another famous example, of course. There were few opportunities open to women at the time: the life of a governess, which Anne Brontë, particularly, chronicles so exactly, must have been humiliating and difficult, though one wonders if the position of nanny in the world we live in now is all that different.

You have a scene in the novel where Charlotte stands outside her father's door, preparing to tell him about Jane Eyre, *but nervous because the novel dares to voice women's desire for love and fulfillment. Meanwhile Emily is terrified by the prospect of being revealed as the author of* Wuthering Heights *because of its passion and honesty. How difficult is it to bare one's soul in print? What fears have you had to overcome as a writer?*

It is always dangerous to write the truth. One ends up upsetting someone. If one looks back at the history of literature, many great writers have run into serious trouble because of their works, from early writers like Corneille to Flaubert, James Joyce, Oscar Wilde, and Nabokov. Also, of course, there are the near and dear one is in danger of offending. Certainly, going back for a fiftieth high school reunion in South Africa, I wondered how I would be received by my classmates after writing *Cracks*, a book about a school reunion with a character named Sheila Kohler in the midst. I have written again and again in more or less veiled terms about my sister's death, which has sometimes brought opprobrium from my brother-in-law's relatives. As a writer I feel obliged to write with emotional honesty. Otherwise there seems little point, but I am aware of the risks in this, as I imagine Charlotte Brontë and particularly Emily, who was such a private person, must have been.

How does Becoming Jane Eyre *fit in with your other books? What themes do you like to investigate in your writing?*

I have often written about power, and how people in power manipulate the weak for their advantage. In this book there is the father, of course, who has lost his position of power to some extent in his weakened state, and the professor with whom Charlotte falls in love in Belgium (this bond, teacher-pupil, is one I have explored often and particularly in *Cracks*), as well as the people for whom Charlotte was obliged to work as a governess, and the couple at Thorp Green for whom Anne and Branwell Brontë worked. There are the women in Charlotte's life: her professor's wife and George Smith's mother, who attempt to manipulate her. I have described both her attraction to these people in power and her struggle to assert her independence and sense of intrinsic worth, a theme that recurs constantly in books like *The Children of Pithiviers* and *Crossways*, and in my first novel, *A Perfect Place*.

Charlotte's father wonders, 'who would want to read something by an obscure parson's daughter, living in a remote region of Yorkshire?'. What is your answer to this question? What is it about Jane Eyre *that has proven to be so timeless?*

I'm not sure I can answer this question completely. Something about the work probably escapes us and remains without definition, but certainly much of the book's appeal lies in the reversal at the heart of so many good stories: the vulnerable position of the poor orphan child, the neglected school girl, and the ignored governess and her ultimate triumph over the blinded Mr Rochester – through love, yes, but also through Jane Eyre's determination to preserve her sense of self-worth, her dignity as a human being equal with any other. 'Who in the world cares for you? Or who would be injured by what you do?' the bigamous Mr Rochester asks her, trying to get her to remain with him, and Jane replies, 'I care for myself.' It is ultimately a moral triumph and one that uplifts the spirit of any reader.

What emotion, lesson, or other experience would you like readers to take from this novel?

As with any book, I would hope to carry the reader away into a strange, mysterious, and different place, one where events are structured satisfyingly into a story, as they are not in life, and at the same time a recognizable and believable place where they could share some of what I have experienced in my own life as well as in Charlotte Brontë's. I hope to be able to give all readers the sense that our emotions, even with a great distance in time and place, are similar, that we are not alone, that we all experience sorrow and suffering, moments of hope and despair, that we are part of a community and our emotions are shared ones. I would hope that by following for a while in the paths that these courageous women took will give courage to the men and women who might take up this book and find in its pages a distraction from their lives, but also a deeper understanding of the human heart.